ATRIA
BOOKS

Dear Reader:

H Mart: your destination for delicious Korean snacks, fresh produce, and run-ins with K-pop idols. Well, at least that's the narrator's experience in *The Band*.

In this smart, satirical literary debut, the narrator meets a recently canceled Korean pop star who's hiding to protect his band's reputation. The narrator is an unhappily married therapist who needs to be needed, and she's fascinated by the handsome idol, so what does she do next? She takes him home, of course.

As outrageous as the premise is, it all somehow works. Christine dilutes the absurdity with viciously funny, stylish prose. Drawing from her background as a Harvard-trained psychologist, she also sprinkles intelligent, eye-opening pop-psychology references throughout this slim novel.

When the protagonist isn't narrating her strange new home life with a K-pop celebrity—much to the confusion of her husband and two children—she exposes the dark underbelly of a music industry that shoves its idols up the highest of mountains but provides no safety net for their fall.

Although K-pop fans will have fun spotting some Easter eggs—I certainly did—you don't have to know anything about this music genre to enjoy *The Band*. Many of you are already—willingly or unwillingly—aware of big fandoms, such as Directioners, Beliebers, and Swifties. However, in this age of toxic digital parasocial interactions, *The Band* proves K-pop fandom might be the most formidable of them all.

Loan Le

Loan Le
Senior Editor

Atria Books | 1230 Avenue of the Americas | New York, NY 10020

THE BAND

— *A Novel* —

Christine Ma-Kellams

ATRIA BOOKS

New York London Toronto Sydney New Delhi

ATRIA
BOOKS

An Imprint of Simon & Schuster, Inc.
1230 Avenue of the Americas
New York, NY 10020

This book is a work of fiction. Any references to historical events, real people, or real places are used fictitiously. Other names, characters, places, and events are products of the author's imagination, and any resemblance to actual events or places or persons, living or dead, is entirely coincidental.

First Atria Books hardcover edition April 2024

ATRIA BOOKS and colophon are trademarks of Simon & Schuster, Inc.

Simon & Schuster: Celebrating 100 Years of Publishing in 2024

For information about special discounts for bulk purchases, please contact Simon & Schuster Special Sales at 1-866-506-1949 or business@simonandschuster.com.

The Simon & Schuster Speakers Bureau can bring authors to your live event. For more information or to book an event, contact the Simon & Schuster Speakers Bureau at 1-866-248-3049 or visit our website at www.simonspeakers.com.

Interior design by Jill Putorti

Manufactured in the United States of America

1 3 5 7 9 10 8 6 4 2

Library of Congress Cataloging-in-Publication Data is available.

ISBN 978-1-6680-1837-8
ISBN 978-1-6680-1839-2 (ebook)

To Luke, Josiah, Everest—You are each my favorite
(don't let any of the others in this dedication tell you otherwise).

"... his desire, when it comes, extinguishes her."

—RACHEL CUSK, *SECOND PLACE*

THE BAND

1

Canceled (Let's Start at the End)

Their first single—people laughed. Perhaps snorted would be more accurate. A quintet of boys, too young to understand protest, yet rapping like they knew the secret—*everything you build will be destroyed, so make it beautiful.* Between the eyeliner and wraparound shades, no one recognized them as the dickheads and nerds from around the way who were neither cute enough for the Seoul girls (who demanded both shoulders and double lids, Eurocentrism at its best) nor brilliant enough for the country teachers at Gwangju to take note.

It's true: the youngest one had just walked his eighth-grade graduation and looked it, but no matter—the rhymes paraded out of his still-small mouth so fast I couldn't tell if he was speaking English or Korean, two languages that have never been confused for each other until The Band made Konglish their mother tongue. Sure, with the exception of their lead, their English was not terrific—not even now, when the world is an older and no wiser place, and every other collaboration of theirs is a pop anthem with some American icon who only does stadium tours. But that was the great forgiveness music afforded: songs demanded their own cadences; in pledging allegiance to its rhythms, other identifiers like age and accent and gender fell away like old skins on a serpent. If I closed my eyes and listened to the latest falsetto bridges the youngest released on Sound-Cloud, I might mistake him for a lady angel.

It was no accident that the oldest was also the "visual." To call Sang Duri "the Hot One" would be a failure of translation, the equivalent of equating schadenfreude with simpler joys. For a boy group with a long lineage of feral female fans, sex was not what they were selling. Like the Fab Four of yore,* a gifted tongue could render a man's looks an afterthought. No matter that the lead recently admitted that those wraparound shades from their debut album were less about appropriating Black fashion and more about hiding his own exceedingly Korean face, which he did not consider his forte. Now they were all beautiful, if for no other reason than the worship they inspired. (Did I mention that half of them were atheists? Two were converted by their lead, whose immaculate command of English after watching a year of MTV convinced them of his singularity in knowing for sure what they themselves could only grasp at. And the other half: the kind of Christian who absolutely believes in storing treasures in heaven but cannot help his Givenchy habit or collection of luxury condos in Hannam-dong with their teak-lined bathrooms and views of the Han River.)

How 22 million Twitter followers—plus threefold that number of additional fans who have a moral, linguistic, age-related, or technical opposition to tweeting—missed the clues to what happened next suggests that we need a God after all, so bad are we at managing our own affairs, or at least those of the ones we love. (By the time I arrived on the scene, it was all a moot point anyway.)

The first hint landed on the day of the eldest's birthday. As was custom, the boys always released a song they'd written themselves

*Paul, John, Ringo, and George.

on the day commemorating their birth. If you find it surprising that this was their idea of a good time, then perhaps you do not understand that to arrive at global domination, a person's primary, if not only, joy must be work. (Ask yourself: When was the last time you reached the pinnacle of anything?)

In it, Duri sings about a boy who jumps into the ocean in the hopes of becoming a fish so that he can see his father, a commercial fisherman who loves his son but loves the sea more. Think *The Little Mermaid* in reverse, without the undercurrent of bestiality and ageism—a sanitized, platonic version of the Disney classic, albeit with a dash of suicide ideation maybe. He titled it something that cannot be translated but loosely means "The Hole."

He admitted on the day of its release: "Strange song for birthday, no?"

If anybody's wondering: the boy in the song succeeds. He lands on his father's liner transformed, his transition successful, wearing nothing but net. He notices the dozen kilo of other fish lying next to him and tries to gauge them for signs of sentience. Are these all his father's sons? He watches a light-skinned yellowtail get chosen by his progenitor for its glass eyes, bulbous and wet. The man on the boat fingers its gills loosely before filleting the thing whole, then carefully slicing the remains into sashimi-sized pieces. The song ends just as fish boy appears to be next.

In the comments section on YouTube, no one explicitly asks if the father goes through with eating his son. Or if the son had an alternative exit strategy in mind.

What they do ask, over and over, is whether the sashimi meant that the father was Japanese. Really, it was hard not to emphasize the utter importance of this determination and all that it implied. Japan's cultural minister preemptively tweeted: "We are not cannibals." The Japanese embassy in Seoul closed for the day, its flag mysteriously gone from its mast.

The Koreans also thought the answer was yes but were not any happier about it. A common refrain: "First they invaded us, now they eat our idols?" Others asked if this meant Duri was a half-breed, and if so, what the hell he was doing being one of South Korea's prime cultural exports? #HONYOL* trended on Twitter. Korean-American hip-hop loyalists inquired: "Why the dad gotta be Japanese?" TikTok got its first East-East history lesson when #chinilpa** went viral for a day, then two.

Even the Chinese, in a bout of either FOMO or nationalism, got into the fray: "WW2 Never Forget," they typed, not needing to reference their Japan conquistadores by name. Not since #MeToo did the word "rape" make it into so many WeChat transcripts (#RapeofNanking***), so much so that the censor-bots put a moratorium on flagging that keyword, serendipitously letting a handful of survivors live another day.

American fans, for our part, kept mum, maybe because being particular to one brand of racism could make a person oblivious to another, or because recent events suggested that we were not one to talk. Although a few brave ones asked in private messages:

Chinese Japanese Korean remind me the difference again?

You mean besides what country

What's their beef

And that was just the start of it.

Behind marbled doors, Duri asked, "Should I disappear?"

The lead, who called himself Min, scoffed or swallowed a winged

---

*"Mixed blood" (i.e., mixed race)

**Technically *chinilpa* means "pro-Japanese collaborator," but for all intents and purposes, what it really translates into is "traitor," a slur so cursed ever since Japan annexed Korea more than a century ago that it still has an illustrious history of canceling the lives of not only those it was levied against but also their children and children's children, because what else are curses good for if not making sons pay for the sins of their fathers?

***Rape of Nanking: I'm not one to dramatize history (who is very good at being its own drama queen) but let me just say this: the brutality Japanese soldiers unleashed on the once-capital of the Republic of China was so gory that it allegedly led a Nazi to wring his hands.

insect—the noise he made could not differentiate—and said, "Your problems, our problems." Then, as if citing this as evidence, he added, "*Tu casa es mi casa.*"

The smartest kid from Gwangju (but evidently not the most brilliant boy in this room) protested, "That's not English or Korean."

"Americans say it all the time," Min assured. "It means we are all together."

"Some of us are more together than others," the youngest one replied. Besides being the primary vocalist and maknae of the group, Jae rapped as well as the primary rappers and competed with the only classically trained dancer of the group for the best body rolls, plus was exceptionally good at flirting with girl bands during awards shows and television appearances, striking that perfect alchemy of competence mixed with warmth—a formula potent enough to ward off both the negative stereotypes associated with *being less than* and the jealousy that comes with being *too good.* Talent is a burden for which the only relief is attention.*

The professional dancer shot him a glance whose effect rivaled that of the most violent of body rolls. His name (Yoojin) easily sounded American (Eugene) if you screamed it out loud and ignored the spelling; for this reason, he was the target of the most explicit DMs from the progressive-minded white girls of Instagram who took their own colorblindness—when it came to matters of penis—to be a sure sign that they were anti-racists making the world a better place, one offer of a Very Good Time (wink wink, peach emoji, eggplant) at a time.

Duri repeated, "I could disappear, no problem."

The sixth person in the room—a guy named Pinocchio—did not say anything. Another clue, maybe? The more powerful a person is, the easier it is for them to simply will their plans into existence, come what may.

---

*But is it paying attention or getting it? That is the question.

2

A Riddle

Here's a riddle that befuddles parents but serves to justify the existence of my entire field of work: When is a child most likely to drown in a swimming pool?

Answer: During a party. Disappearances are most probable in front of an audience.

Funny, then, how a boy could evaporate in a house of five roommates. Then again, crazier things have happened to less-famous people.

The following month, the next album landed on schedule with its requisite string of music videos, each one more avant-garde than the last. By the time the third single hit YouTube, it was unclear to more recent fans whether they were watching a hip-hop Korean boy band perform or a Sundance shorts frontrunner. The Five, intact on screen. Although with CGI, anything is possible. In an unprecedented move, a sushi boat brimming with sashimi made a brief cameo, followed by a surrealist visit to an aquarium overrun by fish. The symbolic equivalent of the middle finger, I think?

Duri, absent suddenly from video uploads and television appearances, afforded The Band a new symmetry. From then on, whenever they appeared live, the boys formed a pair of rows, as if a two-rank-line formation could protect them from the real or imaginary presence of people and their prolonged gazes.

Fan sightings of the former visual in destinations as unlikely as Rio de Janeiro and Marrakech were followed by more conceivable destinations in virtually every metropolis and hamlet except for the ones directly across Seoul's northern border (if the netizens of Pyongyang saw our beloved, no one else heard about it). In a country where military service was still a required rite of passage, there was the idea that perhaps our boy had been drafted into some secretive mission, plucked from one line of service for the purposes of another. Maybe he was on a mental health vacation. Or maybe he was already on the other side of help, when such vacations fail and a traveler is left with finding a more permanent solution to temporary problems. Like any true legend, he was both everywhere and nowhere.

Still, new configurations of his voice belted out of never-before-heard songs. With no impending tour dates scheduled, resolutions were not required.

At one point, Min said out loud to his bandmates, "We don't need the money, you know."

"I have too much Givenchy," Yoojin agreed, perhaps thinking of the competition it posed to his Christianity.

Jae said, "It was never for the money anyway." For this reason, everyone called him by this stage name, which meant either "talent" or "wealth" in Korean, depending on how it was written, which in turn depended on whether people assumed that he was born rich and became an idol for the fame or that he was merely born talented and became one for the money. What they didn't know was that he became an idol because he was no good at anything else; behind every singularity is desperation.

"So, what, it was for the glory?" Yoojin inquired.

"Celebrity is a disease," declared Gwangju's genius, who could read minds but had a hard time recovering from the knowledge. He peered at Jae, squinting. "Out of the five of us, you were the only one who auditioned on your own. Duri got street cast boarding the goddamn train for looking the way he does. Yoojin's dance teacher sent him to Seoul on scholarship to be a trainee. I accompanied my brother to his audition and pretended to be him when he had a panic attack standing in line. We do not talk anymore—"

"Min auditioned—" Jae interjected.

"Min sent a tape of himself riffing on a Drake song at the behest of a fellow street rapper, who also does not talk to him anymore. You see a pattern?"

"Are you accusing me of something?" Jae could not believe it.

"Nobody is mad," Min declared, raising both hands above his head as if there was going to be a vote on the matter and his election could possibly count twice.

"You wanted this," Gwangju said, still looking at Jae. "All by yourself, you wanted it, took the bus to Gangnam from middle school and sang your way through three rounds before getting four offers, one from each of the Big Three agencies, and of course, our own humble producer, with nothing but a disgraced girl group to his name."

"I feel like there is an insult in this somewhere," Jae told Min, who just shook his head.

"The rest of us fell into this. You looked at fame straight in the eye and wanted it," Gwangju explained.

"And that makes me . . . ?"

"Psychologically unwell."

Jae giggled, a little hysterical. Despite being familiar with the stans* who obsessively tracked his hormonal acne (detectable only under conditions of under-makeup or fluorescent light) or commented on whether he was retaining extra water in his latest Instagram posts or drew causal inferences about his mental health based on the number of words uttered during interviews or commented on his pitch or deep-web-searched images of his abs or wished death upon the occasional woman lucky (or unlucky) enough to be caught in a photo with him, he was unused to being insulted by his own hyungs and found the experience to be a tickle.

"You wanted to be famous," Gwangju repeated. "You are the only one of us too young to remember life before the internet and social media, so you know exactly what modern celebrity is like: coming home after a long day's work to a couple million strangers shouting at you in your own living room, from your own bed, on the toilet, whenever, wherever there is a screen and a Wi-Fi connection—"

"It is the price we pay," Min cut in. "Not everyone is so lucky. Are you really complaining?"

Before Gwangju could defend his right to see the future but suffer once he got there anyway, Jae's laughter rolled and roiled, seizure-like and a little concerning even to his accuser, who wondered if perhaps he'd pushed the logical conclusion on this one a bit too far. "The funny thing is . . ." He hiccupped between convulsions. "You are calling me insane—sorry, psychologically unfit—for wanting to be an idol more than the rest of you, but I am the only one not always on the verge of some nervous breakdown or eating disorder. You and

---

*Not to be confused with the equally fair share of diehard fans who merely wished him well and loved him from afar and adamantly refused to speculate on things about which they could say nothing of real value and understood the difference between a famous person they followed versus somebody they actually knew and managed to fill the holes in their lives with God or religion or dick or cocaine or any other number of possible consumables other than a celebrity known as much for their light as their shadow.

Min—and Duri too—are always writing lyrics about depression or anxiety, and Yoojin is always talking about fasting and going to the gym—which, please, do not go well together—so I would say that if your argument is right, it appears that insanity makes for a more psychologically robust person, no?"

Silence, because it was true, until at last Gwangju inquired, "Short of us all going crazy, then, what do you suggest we do?"

"Yoko broke up the Beatles," Min offered, an alternative solution to the problem no one was naming.

"You believe everything you read," Jae accused. And then, "No girl in all of Asia would admit to breaking us up, even if she did or could. Too much responsibility."

"A girl in the West might." Gwangju's orbital muscles contracted, adding two little bows on the corner of each eye. "Might try, I mean," he clarified, looking around at the others, who were not smiling but, still, perhaps their faces or hair color or personal style correlated with their attitudes toward interracial coupling. "If she could do it, she'd probably be very proud of herself. And have no problem announcing it."

"Is this a confession?" Min demanded.

Gwangju cackled, inappropriate affect being his marker and prize. It made him both annoying to his bandmates, who tolerated his displays of emotion with the same forbearance that they extended to each other's sugar gliders and cockatoos, and irresistibly charismatic to total strangers, who could not believe someone that famous could reveal himself with the kind of abandon typically reserved for gods or demagogues. "We all live together," he replied, as if one fact displaced another. "If I—how do you say it?—'hooked to' someone, as they say in America, and liked them enough to consider disbanding us over them, you'd have to be blind not to know about it."

"*Hooked up with,* you mean," corrected Yoojin, who knew far more

English than he let on for no other reason than the freedom that being ignored bought him—a priceless charade for a man who could afford anything except oblivion.

"We date white girls now?" Jae inquired, surprised and a little excited.

"Technically," Gwangju's most notable alum replied, "we do what we want."

Young Jae laughed again, loud and hysterical, a protest unto itself.

Min answered for him. "Everything is permissible, but not everything is beneficial."

"You quoting the Bible now?" asked Yoojin, who was still considering a switch to atheism and trying it on from time to time for its fit.

Ignoring the question, Gwangju said, "Yoko Ono got her latest death threats thirty-six years after she allegedly broke up the Beatles and twenty-six years after John Lennon moved on to the other side. Name the man, woman, or child you'd wish that upon." Perhaps he was thinking about his own wife, a soft-faced civilian whose theoretical existence had long been denied but whose physical body resided in a small, austere loft apartment in Mapo-gu, crosshatched by both an orthodox selection of ninety-degree angles and a liberal commitment to white space.

"Peow," confirmed the dancer. Yoojin pointed his index finger to his temple before collapsing on the ground in a neat little heap like an imperial accordion fan folding upon itself, all hard-earned elbows and knees brought on by his latest bout of intermittent fasting.

Duri, who was not in the room (I can attest as his alibi), called out—or perhaps they just imagined it—"Be careful."

Whether he was referring to the assassination attempts by the women they had yet to meet or their own ability to see the future and run into its arms anyway, these, for the time being, remained empirical questions to be tested.

3

Upon Further Reflection

Turns out, The Band was not really like the Beatles. Apart from their mutual occupation of history, they had little else in common, and for me to compare one with the other would be like using Mother Teresa's extravagant obsession with helping the needy, one leper at a doorstep a day, to draw a simile with Jeff Bezos's lavish, Amazonian pursuit of being able to address people's every need, one package on a porch at a time. An overreliance on parallels makes for a dizzy picture.

The origin stories alone—one born in a Liverpoolian pub in the Occident, the other pieced together by an intentional set of hands in the Orient—necessitated that knowing how things ended or started with Lennon, McCartney, Harrison, and Starr explains little about the way everything unfolded for our little quintet of boys whom everyone thought they knew but really had no idea.

These guys—even long after they were forced to leave childhood behind upon acquiring the many, many zeros in the virtual spaces where real value and worth reside (Hyundai Black cards, subscribers, followers, downloads, likes, fans, stans)—lived in a sanitized dorm where the multitude of load-bearing walls belied its square meterage. Its glossy birch floors eased into the almond-colored ceiling with a kind of seamlessness that could make the sanest person wonder which way is up. Even the laziest archaeological excavation of old memes revealed that such digs were a massive upgrade from their old apartment on the other side of the river with its sooty, mold-colored stucco and excess of twin bunk beds, rich with hope even as it lacked everything else.

The dorm, though, was not the room where the start of The Band happened (of course not).

Picture this with me instead: a man in his forties with a bowl cut and a Pinocchio face—strangely rosy cheeks, a mouth so unnaturally red and shaped that you wonder if it is carved—sitting on his velveteen couch. Ignore, for a moment, his paunch—a dead giveaway to his age—and his underwear—Calvins, yes, but in an in-between color that leans toward either buttercup under the incandescent bulbs of his lampshade or reptilian gray under the fluorescent tubes directly behind his television screen. He is crying over a porcelain bowl of jajangmyeon, the tears salting the already salty black noodles and doing no favors for his namesake bloat, one that he wears proudly and without shame, which says something about his stature, his power, his impending omnipotence. A true sign of a king is his figure—or more accurately, the complete irrelevance of his figure.

Duran Duran is on the screen, Simon Le Bon looking like a supremely well-dressed Jesus surrounded by hordes of brown children, singing in his characteristic doublespeak that, like so many Christian songs, makes it impossible to tell whether he is talking about sex or religion. "Save a prayer 'til the morning after," he warbles. Our man is gripping a dog-eared manga between his knees—who needs a gratitude journal when there is Naruto to save you?—but he is not reading, only staring at Le Bon, startled that a one-night stand with a woman never to be seen again could move a white guy to write a love song as devastating as this. Something about the broken arpeggio, tagging along the D and B minor chords, pairs with the ever-slippery bass to remind us that the first and last songs uttered by man are always ones of lament.

Could this be the secret chord Leonard Cohen croons about in "Hallelujah?" The *minor fall*, the *major lift*—our baffled king composes no hymns that night but wonders what sorcery could lead himself, a naked middle-aged South Korean fellow, fat and sated, to sob over a bowl of what is now essentially soup. It's not just the lyrics or the tune or even the alchemy of startlingly good looks scrambled with art school edge and punk rock ethics. More likely, it is something far simpler and true: Duran Duran figured out that all art is story; the only musicians we remember are the raconteurs.

Our man—I like to call him Pinocchio—becomes an impresario that night: first in his head, then In Real Life. First, though, he needs to commit suicide.

The next morning, in Gangnam-du, the only neighborhood in Seoul that Americans know thanks to Psy's surprise techno-pop hit heralding "Gangnam Style," in an office bedazzled with both natural light and album covers featuring the most artificial of lighting conditions, the impresario is facing another man. His counterpart is Korean and middle-aged like him, but thinner and better-looking, with a face sculpted more from stone than dough. He is not handsome technically, but composed of familiar features reminiscent of other faces we've seen before, like a friendly Frankenstein.

"It's over for me," Pinocchio says. "I'm leaving. Consider this my notice."

His counterpart looks at him and says his real name. It sounds like a reprimand, although the misdeed has yet to be named. "Whatever I've done, remember that we are not in America anymore, trying to convince miguksaram* to listen to K-pop and disturbing each

---

*미국사람—i.e., Yankees

other with our bad habits. Even there, when you got mad at me over the laundry or the things I suggested trainees do, do you remember what you did?"

"I left."

"Correction: You left and then came back. You walked a lap around the block and returned to our shitty little apartment because there was nowhere else to go. Today, you are also free to walk around the neighborhood. Go get a churro. Walk as long as you like. Then and now, there is nowhere else to go."

"The story of the Omelas,"* Pinocchio replies.

Frankenstein only shakes his head; no need to embarrass himself by confirming or denying whether he knows what the hell his buddy is talking about. "There are two things you love more than I do. Three, actually. Books, eating, and anime. This explains why you are smart but I am likable, you are fat but I am trim, you are a bachelor and I am not. I admit these freely, along with my weakness over unfolding socks. Satisfied?"

Our man Pinocchio presses on. "The Omelas live in a beautiful, sweet city. They are happy. Technically they are, no one debates this. But there is a child that lives underground somewhere in the city, a little boy full of shit and cornmeal, and everyone knows all about it, and they also know that keeping the child there makes the city possible."

"We got rid of slave contracts; you know that as well as me." Frankenstein glances at the posters of single-gendered bands in matching, monochromatic costumes and polychromatic hair. "There are no children chained to us here, making our existence possible. Every idol gets a cut, and the cuts now are bigger than they ever were."

---

*Long before the *New Yorker* made viral short stories an actual thing (see: Kristen Roupenian's "Cat Person"), there was Ursula Le Guin and her wildly popular 1973 allegory about the Omelas. It won a Hugo; it proved that women could write sci-fi and that the genre could be about something more than white guys going off to conquer alternate universes.

Pinocchio shakes his head. "This is not an accusation. The point is, there is nothing beyond the Omelas, only darkness. Even so, somebody in the story keeps walking anyway, walks away even in the absence of somewhere to go."

"Are you depressed?" Frankenstein inquires, suspicious of the two separate conversations each person in this scene seems to be having.

"Suicidal, maybe, but not sad."

"Career suicide, you're talking about."

"If it was actual suicide, you think I would be here, telling you about it beforehand?"

"This could be a cry for help."

"This is a courtesy because before we were producers, we were roommates, and before we were roommates, we were friends. I am mad, but not at you. Music is a zero-sum game where winner takes all, which, sadly, ruins both winners and losers the way lottos ruin both the cursed man who gets the jackpot and all the cursed men who do not. I have to do something else, or else do things differently."

"You are right on both accounts. But you also have no plans," Frank ("Frankenstein" is such a mouthful, no?) guesses.

"For the moment, no. I do not have a plan. I hope to do music till the day my Type-A personality culminates in a heart attack and instant death."

"Okay." Frank smiles because he is sure this is not how this story ends. If a prince could not give up his princely riches for the kingdom of Heaven with the son of God making the sale himself, it is unlikely that a fat, sentimental man with a taste for processed foods (prepared by any hands except his own) can leave behind the only job he's ever gotten paid for by the only industry he's ever loved for a life teetering on the edge of poverty and oblivion. Unlikely and improbable, yes, but not impossible, not a probability of zero, and as any empiricist will tell you, the road to error is paved with the bones of people who do not understand statistics.

Pinocchio walks out into the sunlight, where the air is wet and characteristically summer for Seoul. As a testament to his humanity, he does get a churro. It is as much of a concession of his once and future best friend (when, down the line, The Band makes him an even richer man than the partner he left behind) as a nod to his own belly. At the snack bar incomprehensibly named after the mental capacity of someone with below-average intelligence—IQ84 Churros Cafe—he orders a classic one. In his hands, it is warm and smells of honeyed butter. He realizes just now that it is shaped like a noose, the striated fried dough forming a perfect loop, albeit one that ends in a narrow containment of seams and not a knot, a nod to the existence of tomorrows. He takes a bite, then another. It is good; it is very good. Sometimes a man doesn't need much.

The churro, of course, is not enough, even though Pinocchio gets another one the following morning. He is first in line. If I had to guess: he is there before the tourists and the natives alike, before even the shopkeeper himself cranks open the awning window and reheats yesterday's peanut oil. We cannot blame him, because leave it to South Koreans to bastardize the best of Spain's and Mexico's trademark pastry and combine them into one glorious donkey of a snack. These churros flaunt the girth and cinnamon sugar coating of the Mexican variety conjoined with the decadent chocolate sauce that necessarily accompanies the Spanish ones. Then they're souped up with enough customization options—cream cheese or sour cream, mango and/or ice cream, Nutella with or without nuts?—to make a man forget that he ever needed anything else.

Frank, though, is right about the poverty and oblivion. For the next eight years, Pinocchio cobbles together one disastrous music group after another in search of his magnum opus. Chemistry is not the only study of change. On this, Walter White is only partially right and completely Eurocentric. While high school chemists crane over their beakers and meth lords in hazmat suits turn cold remedies mixed with battery acid into moon dust, the great Republic of Korea is figuring out how to win friends and influence people by churning their young into the kind of irresistible music groups the rest of the world can't get enough of. Their target: China, Japan, and the U.S., before moving on to India, the Philippines, and everywhere else, one prepubescent hopeful at a time.

Unlike Frank and other producers, though, Pinocchio has no interest in being a puppet master. He likes—no, loves—music too much to want to tell the people who make it precisely how to do it and when, or under what exact conditions. True love demands freedom. Both God and the devil intuited this after the initial Bang and the first rib removal, despite having no experience whatsoever with human beings and their squirrelly ways. Both powers-that-be seem to understand that choice is a prerequisite to anything worth sticking around for. Maybe they, like our impresario, also just want to see what will happen if you let people do what they desire.

Arguably, God, the devil, and Pinocchio all see what is coming and still manage to appear surprised by it.

4

The Unnamed Unfortunate Event

alamity comes first. The year before The Band ejects themselves from the safe but austere womb of being trainees, Pinocchio debuts a girl group who shall not be named. Voldemort they are not, but you would not be able to tell this by following the trail of tears they leave behind.

The femme trio is—no one debates this—the impresario's first grand idea that has a chance of actually working. Titrating New World (read: American) hip-hop with Old World soul, he handpicks a skateboarder, a break-dancer, and a poet to resurrect the OGs of K-pop—The Kim Sisters*—albeit with more of everything: Hangul, sass, skin. They are uniformly beautiful (of course) but actually resemble their ancestors in ways that no girl idol of Frank's ever did because Pinocchio declined to calculate their head-to-body sizes**

---

*Who spoke no English but nevertheless managed to appear on *The Ed Sullivan Show* twenty-two times and break into the Billboard charts thanks to a combination of phonetics, God-given talent, hard work, and extra-tight outfits.

**The golden ratio apparently? To fit at least eight of your heads in your body.

and record their height in centimeters* and conjure up the letter of the alphabet their chin most resembled** and determine whether their complexion reminded him of teeth or cake.*** With their varying jawlines and ratios and Scoville ratings, they look different enough to not be confused for each other during interviews by their fellow countrymen (in other words, among people who understand instinctually that not all Asians look alike) yet who also share one singularity: the ability to rap.

In their debut single, they jump on cars in the middle of one of Seoul's many indistinguishable intersections and incite an impromptu party among hordes of stuffy middle-class netizens just trying to make it home at an hour reasonable enough to not be yelled at by those they love, or are at least stuck with for the time being. Between all the popping and locking, they wax poetic about themselves in one metaphor after another: snakes leaving behind their caskets of old skin; pink apple blossoms enclosing into themselves to become the black, toxic core of an apple fruit; tadpoles giving up their tails for the chance to jump with two feet. It's an instant hit. Pinocchio celebrates with churros and miyeok-guk (birthday soup) even though it is not his birthday.

The grown-ups in the room don't get the song. They say: these girls, they talk too fast; it's gibberish; also, Koreans don't rap; and whatever happened to respecting your elders and not stepping on their cars? A few meticulous fans psychoanalyze the lyrics and wonder aloud if by "I'ma go home with her," the call-and-response refrain is suggesting a girl-on-girl relationship or (gasp!) maybe even a lesbian hookup.

---

*To be at least 165 cm—the American equivalent of almost 5'5", which is a good inch taller than even the average American woman.

**V, of course.

***Ivory or vanilla, take your pick. If you don't believe me, you've never tried finding your shade in a Korean foundation lineup.

No matter. Kids eat it up. They blare it loudly from their laptops when their parents are stuck in traffic and then quietly, with the closed captioning on, when their adults come home. The revelatory tunes sound just wrong enough coming from their mother tongue. Without any actual cussing or direct calls for insurrection or explicit references to one-night stands, the grown-ups cannot find any precedent for banning the song. It lives on airways and playlists for days, then weeks.

By week three on K-pop Hot 100, the girls take a subway ride just to see if they'll get recognized.

"Let's wear hats," the skateboarder suggests, holding up a particularly ugly array of surplus baseball caps she got from a cousin on last year's birthday, easily the nicest gift she has ever gotten from any blood relative (with the exception of maybe life itself).

"I thought the whole point is to get recognized?" asks the break-dancer. Boarding can be a solitary art, performed alone in alleys and in near poverty, but dancing is almost always a group endeavor (historically even a mating call) that requires a minimum degree of money and self-esteem. It is no surprise that these two had fundamentally different ideas about whether fandom is the entire point of what they are doing or just another annoying stop on the way to buying your mother (and that nice cousin) a house.

"We could all go separately," the poet suggests. "If we go as a group, it's too obvious." As someone who lives off words for a living, she has a natural capacity for solitude that neither dancer nor boarder can stomach.

"I'll wear a hat." The break-dancer quickly grabs a dun-colored one. Better to be ugly and attached than pretty and alone; this much is obvious.

Maybe it's the headgear that makes them look like more ordinary versions of themselves. Maybe it's the time of day that makes for an audience unlikely to care about idols. Maybe it is a more sinister act of chart manipulation involving releasing debut acts between the hours of zero and three a.m. to lower the bar for domination that makes them think they are perhaps more popular than they actually are. Regardless, the underground ride proves a waste of three round-trip metro tickets.

When they report this to Pinocchio, he replies, "You idiots." Somehow it sounds worse because he is not yelling but saying it very calmly, almost quietly, like a threat. "Do you not understand? You are not famous yet. No one cares what you had for breakfast or what you are wearing. They do not recognize you or know how different from them you are. So your number one goal in life is to convince everyone that you are not like them. You are unique! In a country not historically known for overvaluing uniqueness!" By now he is yelling, but it does not feel much better.

"Wait a year, after two albums and a tour, then go on the fucking subway, and when you get caught, when kids whip out their phones and take photos and post it online and tag you on Twitter, then it will be a thing. Then it will be publicity. Right now it is nothing. Absolutely nothing. A waste of 3,750 won, 1,250 per metro ticket times three. Let us hope nobody recognized you because if they did, you just lost their fandom. You showed your cards and made yourself one of them before they had a chance to idolize you. You effectively made it impossible for yourselves to be anything other than three girls who can't afford to not ride the subway."

"There is the matter of the trainee debt," the poet says. It is true then (although no longer now, when what happens next to the girls will save The Band from a similar indentured servitude): somebody has to pay for room and board and meals necessary during the protracted auditions and probationary period that stretch out over months and years, not to mention the singing lessons and dance instruction and personal trainers and stylists and, yes, sometimes even the occasional (or not so occasional, depending on the particular moral stance of the agency) blepharo-, epicantho-, lateral cantho-, mento-, genio-, or rhinoplasty.* American acts, perhaps as an extension of the country's youth or stubborn individualism or God-given oblivion, get away with sending out demo tapes and lining up shitty gigs at clubs, courting chance and believing that sparkling self-esteem can stand up to the caprices of dumb luck. South Korean hopefuls, maybe because of their geolocation (in the East) or recent brushes with the hard hand of fate (between being ruled by the Japanese from the annexation of 1910 until World War II to being sawed in half by the Soviets and the Americans after the war), do not believe in chance. They do not rely on the favor of God but do believe in natural selection, in cold hard effort as the only antidote to failure (of history, of God, of Americans).

Maybe because he is a purist or maybe because he's been called ugly himself one too many times, Pinocchio himself does not subscribe to interventions of the plastic-surgery kind. When it would come to his own (future) girlfriends (when his next act— The Band—makes him rich enough to be finally able to afford as many as he desires), he will be as predictable and boring as the rest:

---

*Blepharoplasty: standard double-eyelid surgery to give Asians a fold where no fold exists. Think origami for the face.

Epicanthoplasty: inner corner eyelid surgery to remove the dreaded "Mongolian fold" and reveal the itty-bitty dot of pink tissue where cornea meets skin. Who knew corners could be so sexy?

Lateral canthoplasty: outer corner eyelid surgery to slice your eyelid laterally and thereby reveal more white of the eye, achieving that ever elusive (white) baby doll look.

Mento/genioplasty: chin surgery. To create a chin where there was no good chin or to eliminate a chin where there was too much of one. Apparently, anyone who says "God don't make mistakes" has clearly never been to a plastic surgeon's office.

Rhinoplasty: Westerners have been requesting to break their nasal bones down to resemble ski-slopes for approximately as long as ski slopes have been around, and for just as long, Asians have been requesting augmentation, augmentation, augmentation! Of the bridge, mind you, while simultaneously reducing the width of the nostrils. If you've never thought about the narrowness of your nostrils until now, this would be a good time to go check.

opting for the all-important crease above startlingly round doll eyes, the trim but well-defined aristocratic nose, the slender fox's chin, all against a backdrop whose lack of melanin is rivaled only by its lack of pores. For now, as an involuntary bachelor with nothing to lose and the world to gain, he can afford to take his chances with rarer kinds of beauty. His kind flickers as a function of the lighting and sleep and the sodium content of last night's dinner and who's looking. It is impossible to achieve with a surgeon's scalpel: stark monolids against rounded cheeks, a tiny mound of a nose, along with enough variation in skin tone among the three to suggest that his trio of choice fruits did not all fall from the same family tree. That Pinocchio lets these girls keep their original bones and cartilage just means that on everything else, he expects near perfection, delivered with a smile on the intact faces that their mothers gave them.

"If I see or hear about your three heads together in public again at anything other than an award or variety show, looking for attention, I am—" And here the impresario stops. Three girls plucked from secondary school, who spent all of puberty with neither parents nor boys to prep for this life they are now on the precipice of—what could he take from them other than that which would kill him also? He says, "Apologize to me now."

"We are sorry," they reply in unison, as if having practiced.

He nods and they leave. In retrospect, he should've asked more questions.

The Unfortunate Event happens a year in, shortly after the completion of the girls' debut tour, which starts in Seoul and ends in Southern California. Ten cities, half of which are located in North America (or at least its English-speaking subdivisions; sorry, Mexico!). When the press release for the tour lands on Frankenstein's desk, the more handsome producer calls his old friend and says, in lieu of hello, "You have lost it completely."

"You are talking about my mind, is it?" Pinocchio inquires.

"What else?"

"A debut tour *is* a bit unusual—"

"Unheard of, for a reason—"

"And America—"

"San Jose, Fort Worth, Vancouver, Chicago. Plus, a free show in Los Angeles. Really?" A pause, before Frankenstein notes, "New York is missing."

"Proof that my mind is working after all. Madison Square Garden I'm saving for the future. I'm a man of faith, not an idiot."

"You believe in God now?" Frank asks, surprised. But he admits, "I started attending Bible study myself."

"I heard you joined a cult," corrects his friend. It was on the bottom of the landing page of koreaboo.com, right above the article on his girl group's upcoming "worldwide tour," which tells you something about how Americentric the rest of the world can be.

"I heard you lost your goddamn mind."

"In that case, we must be in the same boat."

A long silence, before this offer comes from Frank: "I have some friends in LA, a former idol trying his hand at commercials and independent movies, you know. I can make the introduction if you think it would be of any use."

"You are better at self-promotion than I am," Pinocchio tells him.

"The last three things you said to me are all insults. Can I not help a friend?"

"Make the introduction, then. I will not stop you. If I remember, I'll thank you later, okay?"

Riddle: Who is more likely to become an enemy, a friend or a stranger?

Answer: The opposite of love is not hate, but indifference.

It is a testament to Pinocchio's innocence (remember this, when the temptation to blame him for everything that happens afterward to both this group and the one to follow overwhelms) that he did not question Frankenstein's intentions or his commitment to their bond as once-bros, roommates, producers. See also—

BIRGing (Basking in Reflected Glory): a psychological process wherein one person celebrates another person's achievements via association as fans, friends, or lovers. Originally used to explain a sports fan's indiscriminate and irrational use of the phrase "we won" to refer to the success of their favorite group of strangers doing something he (it was almost always a he) could never do himself. Here's the problem with psychology: BIRGing is a thing, but not everyone does it. The real question is: Who BIRGes and who doesn't?

The former idol: Let me give him a name. Not his real one, for reasons that will be obvious soon enough to anyone who has ever had to deal with lawyers. I will call him Gun, because that's what he is: a weapon, wielded by someone else, to shred whatever object crosses his path.

His looks we should get out of the way. In stories about to be as scandalous as this one, people always really need to know what all the players involved look like. It is less about putting a face to a name and more about deciding who to blame. Ever notice attractive people are less likely to be found guilty? (If not, see: The Halo Effect; more on this later). Casey Anthony, Jeremy Meeks, O. J. Simpson: They probably all did it; we just got too distracted. Shame on us for having eyes that see. In the case of Gun, he is not quite as good-looking as the five members of The Band, but he has what many middle-aged married women commonly refer to as the "Good Father Face." It is a set of features prevalent among American presidents but not domestic or foreign dictators: a pronounced but not too flashy jaw line—one that goes on for hours but not days—eyes that twinkle rather than pierce, no facial hair to speak of but a strong pair of brows, a baseline degree of bilateral symmetry. That is part of the problem: all averages are true, but no average is true of everyone.

The day Pinocchio and his girls descend onto the same concrete tarmac of LAX that a solo Duri will grace a fistful of years later, the horizon is thick with both smog and potential—the only two constants in the occasionally hellish City of Angels. With their bucket hats and massive shades and hardshell Samsonite luggage, they manage to look like every other Asian in the terminal, made interchangeable by their shared fears of the sun and the weather. (Likely this, too, is how their more famous male descendant will manage to infiltrate the American frontier's busiest airport without so much as a single paparazzi shot or unauthorized selfie betraying his coordinates: with an abundance of headgear and no telltale entourage, the most famous Asian man alive in the free world just might pass for any other.)

On this particular morning, Gun surprises Pinocchio and his trio by showing up at baggage claim with a box of Asian pears and three bouquets of orchids in a family of related hues. He hands the flowers out indiscriminately to the three women—the fruit goes to the impresario, of course—but then Gun steps back to assess his choices. The purple dendrobiums have gone to the skater, whose body suggests sex and whose face suggests a second opinion. She carries the universally beloved proportions of a highly fertile woman (snatched waist, voluminous ass, tits to match, plus the elongated limbs of a much skinnier female) and facial features too rare to be considered a standard beauty: eyes shapely but small, like those of some exotic species of cat, studded upon a heart-shaped but otherwise flat face, so flat it conjures up the plains of Kansas. Did he want to fuck her then or merely stare? We'll never know.

What we do know is this: The pink phalaenopsis have gone to the break-dancer, their fuchsia petals serendipitously matching her neon pink ensemble of boxy sweatshirt meets even roomier pants, a getup designed by birth to hide whatever lies beneath and therefore avoid all future possibility of judgment, positive and negative alike. It works; Gun does not dwell a second on her figure but only looks her straight in the eye, nodding respectfully as if she were a fellow man. He moves on to the poet, who receives the color-enhanced royal-blue bouquet with a funny look on her doll face—all eyes and cheeks, with almost no room left for mouth and nose, giving her an uncanny quality, as if she were the avatar of someone else. She is holding the blooms gingerly between her fingers when she quietly observes, "What alien outpost are these from?"

"She means 'thank you,'" Pinocchio interjects before introducing himself. Meeting strangers for the first time has that effect on him— making him temporarily prone to giving shits and weirdly defensive of classic collectivist norms of group harmony. "We were not expecting you. Did Frank tell you our flight schedule?"

"It's nothing, nothing at all. I'm not doing anything today. I just stopped by Han Ah Reum* on my way here, no trouble," Gun replies.

"These are from the grocery store?" the poet presses. "Ajummas don't buy flowers on a regular basis. The ones here do?"

The two other women toss her a sharp look, but it's unnecessary. Gun, like a good number of his fellow countrymen, is used to ignor-

---

*If you've ever wondered what the H in H Mart stands for, now you know. But for the conspiracy minded, what may really cook your noodle is this: While there are a grand total of nine H Marts in the greater Los Angeles area primed to meet the psychosomatic needs of any Asian with a hankering for home (a need that can only be conquered gastronomically, through eating the food you grew up on), the one closest to LAX remains its outpost on the Pacific Coast Highway at the base of a sleepy residential hill aptly named Palos Verdes, where Dispatch and TMZ do not reach, and a man (a boy?) with nowhere to hide can lose himself for a few (hours or days or maybe, just maybe, a lifetime). After all, in both Seoul and the City of Angels, food markets are historically the only reliable places where our Sang Duri can wander unafraid because people are just looking to sate their most primordial needs. When they're hungry, no one is looking for their favorite international pop star. If you don't believe me, consider this: When was the last time you saw someone's selfie with a celebrity in a grocery store?

ing comments he has no intention of addressing. "You look tired," he observes, although this insult is directed at no particular woman, just hangs in the air for whoever feels most insecure about their looks. "I've made plans to take you out tonight. Take a nap first."

"I'm S," the skater says. He has not asked, but she can tell he wants to know what to call her. He'll need this info for later. She bows deep enough for him to see the top of her crown and its thin alabaster line of scalp. "This is Kimme." Straightening back up, she nods to the dancer. "And our resident songstress, her name is Ilee."

Gun dips his torso in return and says, "I'd introduce myself, but I think you know my name already."

At this, Ilee replies, "All the girls had photocards and pillow dolls of you in secondary school."

"Did all the girls include you?" A loaded question such as this upon meeting someone for the first time is usually a bad sign; I think this much is obvious.

Ilee proves to be a killer herself. "I am here in Los Angeles for our debut tour and they are not. It doesn't matter whether they included me or not, does it?"

Pinocchio looks exasperated. If you want to know the precise facial expression he has on, look up the scene in Mary Shelley's book where her Modern Prometheus discovers that his Creature is, in fact, alive as intended. He recovers enough to interject again. "You're the veteran here. We have much to learn from you. I do not think anyone thought K-pop could travel overseas until you did it. Frank takes all the credit for sending you to China and Japan, but even Asians in America caught wind of you—that's how the legend goes. Did he ever tell you that the two of us first came to Los Angeles because you moved here, and we wanted to see what the market was for other acts?"

Gun bristles. His lower jaw shifts ever so slightly against his teeth, like tectonic plates rubbing. "An inauspicious start. I heard that was the trip that broke the two of you up."

"I quit to start my own production company."

"Look at you now, your first debut group on their first debut tour, in America already. How envious is Frank? Did he say?"

Pinocchio looks surprised because those who are pure of heart also tend to be the biggest fools; innocence and ignorance have gone hand in hand since the creation of sheep. "He has his own lineup. What is there to envy?"

"A man always wants what he doesn't have." Gun is looking at S as he says this. No one but Ilee notices. He lifts his right hand, gesturing toward the sliding exit doors, flashing the titanium band on his fourth finger, and the four Koreans follow him into the thick Angeleno sunlight heavy with both emissions and opportunity, unprepared for what is about to come next.

5

Chateau Marmont

How does the old saying go? When a person shows you who they are, believe them the first time? When I saw Maya Angelou first give this advice to Oprah at three o'clock one summer in 1993, neither the three Korean girls in this story nor the progenitor who birthed both them and The Band were around a television screen to hear it. Even if they were, none of them spoke English yet or were worldly enough to appreciate the wisdom of an older woman who has seen some shit.

If they had, it might've helped. Said advice would hint at what kind of man Gun is capable of being by virtue of what he is driving when the five of them traverse the concrete jungle of LAX's many crosswalks and parking structures to arrive at his car. If a girl's face tells you everything a person needs to know about her reproductive abilities,* then a boy's ride will tell you how he'll treat you before, during, and after the act. This one is none other than a Dodge Viper, made during a year when Chrysler still manufactured them to

---

*Studies show: you can tell how fertile a woman is just by looking.

address their long-standing self-esteem issues as an American car company making motorsports racers for drivers of average ability at best. It is red, that specific shade of cherry reserved for lipstick and sports cars. Even Pinocchio can't help but raise a single bushy eyebrow upon seeing the cartoon of a vehicle, all nose and engine.

Ilee is the first to break the quiet hum of roller bags spiraling against asphalt by laughing a short little snort, loud and abrupt. "This is your car?"

Gun stops and conjoins his palm with his forehead. "I forget it only has room for two. I only purchased it last week, silly me. I should've brought the Camaro; it seats four . . ."

At the mention of America's second-most douchey car, Pinocchio's other eyebrow ascends toward heaven. Either that or he is embarrassed for Gun that his numbers still don't match up (one host + three girls + their producer = five seats needed, not four). And you thought Asians were supposed to be good at math.

". . . It's a shame, truly, shame on me. Three of you will have to call a cab, I suppose, but one can ride with me. . . ." Gun blabbers on.

"It is our fault for imposing," Pinocchio suggests, although no one believes it.

"S, you want to?" Gun is already standing by the passenger door, arms resting on the illegally tinted windows, further proof of his questionable capacity to do the right thing and not break something in the process (in this present case, the California Highway Patrol laws; in the future, a person and her band).

S looks at the other girls warily, but they are already backing away from the Viper, the furious whirling of their luggage wheels reverberating through the parking structure. Pinocchio is even farther, although before he disappears into the elevator doors on the other side, he calls out, "Hotel Marmont, remember that! This first night only."

One yellow cab, two prolonged hours, and three crisp Jacksons later, Pinocchio and his remaining two girls are scooting up the lacquered steps of LA's most storied chateau for the DIY photoshoot documenting the girls' first trip abroad. Armed with the latest iPhone, whose enhanced camera modalities threaten to put professional photographers out of business, he is planning on undertaking it himself. Only upon swiping his credit card for incidentals—no Gun or S in sight yet—is he informed by the front desk staff that, in fact, the hotel has a strict no-photography policy enforced with the same level of zeal that Americans reserve for religion and partisan politics.

"Four hundred a night and I cannot take photo?" he demands of the ever-smiling man behind the counter. Then, as if this changes anything: "You know K-pop? The girls, they are famous band in Korea."

The concierge does not bother to look at Kimme or Ilee to assess for recognition because no, he does not know K-pop *yet* and cannot predict the future day when he will have no choice in the matter. "We treat celebrities no differently," he declares, the most outrageous lie he has told in a job already brimming with fables. Even in a country founded on the premise that all men are created equal, there are few things that America can agree on more than the specialness of the rich, famous, or preternaturally talented. If said talent hails from some other part of the world, on the other hand, everyone gets treated as an equal, meaning, a nobody. The opposite of a somebody is an egalitarian.

Pinocchio does not argue—the Free World has made him tame; it has this effect on Asians, has anyone noticed?—only takes the keys and leads the two girls across the crowded lobby well-populated with both tufted furniture and celebrity voyeurs but surprisingly devoid of actual celebrities. The voyeurs do not stare when the three Koreans pass them on the way to the elevator because hello, this is the late aughts; at this prolonged moment in time, the only famous Asians in town are Lucy Liu and Lisa Ling, whom most people cannot tell apart anyway and therefore do not bother trying to recognize (see: outgroup homogeneity effects).

In their rooms, all three hundred square feet each, Pinocchio examines the handwritten note addressed to him on the embossed stationery perched in a tray of ordinary fruit—a bruised banana, an undersized clementine, a Bartlett pear with the leaves still attached—and wonders if this personal touch is enough to warm him up after the chill of the reception desk. Next door, Kimme is busy rubbing her hands furiously against the cashmere throws guarding the matching double beds while Ilee is in the bathroom cross-examining the brands and sizes of the surfactants on the counter. She has never heard of the Chateau Marmont before, but she does know this: You can always tell how nice a hotel is by what precisely they are willing to give away for free. Free parking and complimentary breakfasts are red flags, indicators of a low star count, but free bottles of luxury American-made hair and body products (Kiehl's in this case) means somebody is doing something right. She pockets the lotion (sorry, the *crème de corps*)—a future gift for her umma—but leaves the shampoo/conditioner and body wash to avoid raising the suspicions of her bandmates.

The exhaust-fueled notes of a V8 engine bring both parties to the window, where even the ambient street noise of Sunset Boulevard is not sufficient to mask the low vroom of the incoming Viper, all gasoline and emission and no class. S opens her own door, and when she does this, the chorus line from Gun's own single from his idol days wafts out. It sounds like pure sugar, spun to resemble a melody, weirdly derivative of some jingle no one can place and a punchy techno beat that everyone can.

Kimme dangles the cashmere throw out the window and yells, "You've got to come up and feel this." By the time S looks up to place the sound of a familiar voice yelling at her in her native tongue, Gun and his car are gone.

Upstairs, S does what Kimme suggests and responds, "It feels like a small furry animal died to make this blanket. Can we keep it?"

"The price listed on the desk says four hundred American dollars," Ilee points out.

Kimme drops it upon doing the math and conversion to just over 524,000 South Korean won. S and Ilee don't loosen their fingers. Instead, they each stare at the other person until one of them—doesn't matter who—declares, "I won't tell him if you don't."

S waits until dinner to announce that she has plans. In fact, all of them do. They are sitting at the newly opened taco joint across the street from the Chateau—whose own fine dining with its many-dollar-sign rating is out of the question for an almost-famous debut group with more fans than actual money—where the pink drink umbrellas match the pink pickled onions that indiscriminately garnish every dish. Pinocchio is slurping a coral-orange margarita from a decapitated pineapple when he registers S's announcement. His face falls.

"I thought we're just here for drinks. You didn't want us to eat this, did you?" S asks.

Our man can't argue. Despite being a purist who believes that true art needs a minimum degree of freedom, certain idol practices are too functional to ignore. Among them include a tightly reined diet governed by elaborate lists of forbidden fruits—anything with excess salt (too much bloating), nightshades (tomatoes, peppers, eggplant—too inflammatory), dairy (too much lactose)—in other words, all the food groups upon which (gringo) tacos are built.

"Gun is picking us up in his Camaro," S elaborates. "But it only seats four, remember?"

"Unbelievable, this guy," says Pinocchio.

"He's your friend, I thought."

"Correction: he is the friend of a friend. In Korea, I would know what that means, but in America, who knows what that makes him?"

On this, he is right: Hitler was friends with Lord Londonderry, who was friends (of the cousinly variety) with Churchill.

"I don't have to go," offers the poet, because she is a good judge of character. Albeit not, as she is going to prove later, a good judge of the law.

"Do not be ridiculous," says our man, who prefers to eat alone anyway, with the television on. "You three go. I am going back to the hotel."

He does, thank God; they do, unfortunately. That night is the beginning of the end for one band, albeit just the start for another.

6

What Happens at Le Cinq Stays at Le Cinq

Gun shows up on the kitty corner where Marmont Lane diverges from Sunset a full—count them—twenty-five minutes late, which means our trio of femmes fatales spends nearly a half hour rubbing their naked arms or clenching their exposed thighs (but not both; much to my disappointment, there's rules regarding what a self-respecting woman can get away with wearing on any day other than Halloween*) in the clammy Angeleno evening gloom, unprepared for the local reality that along coastal California cities, day and night are two different seasons and thus require entirely different wardrobes. People say that LA doesn't have true winters, autumns, springs, or summers; they forget that winter arrives daily between the hours of sunset and sunrise, whereas the other three seasons split the hours when the sun shines haphazardly among themselves as an undisclosed function of what month

---

*Rules that some of us believe—rightly or not—are meant to be broken, until we do, and something bad occurs, and afterward we can't help but join the chorus of people whispering: What did you *think* was going to happen?

it is, allowing any day in June, because of its gloom, to be colder than a day in December.

Because this will come up later, what each girl wears for their final night on Earth as intact people needs to be fully dissected. S, because she can, has on a blazer necessary for making the rest of her outfit morally acceptable (a tube top bandaged above a pair of skorts, both in the same arctic shade of polar bear). Kimme, because she is both more conventionally attractive and afraid of the situations that being attractive tends to land her in, looks like something out of an art school catalog or maybe the first season of *Top Model*, when the contestants are still trying to outmaneuver one another in the novelty department for a chance to retain their coveted spot in reality television: an expanse of stiff colorless fabric, pleated, pinched, scrunched, and wrapped asymmetrically around her torso to expose a single shoulder like some costumer designer's period piece, if that period started in ancient Greece and ended with the Founding Fathers. She pairs it with a demure pair of houndstooth pants, high-waisted and tailored, to remind everyone of her irreproachable waist-to-hip ratio.*

Ilee, because her anime face is her moneymaker and the primary cause of prolonged staring, goes fully reckless in what can be best described as a deconstructed tuxedo: shirtdress with the collar fully buttoned but nothing underneath or below—just an irreverent pair of Converse—adorned only with a skinny tie worn lariat-style.

No one cares or notices what Gun is wearing. At his age (thirty-five), given his marital status (married, unfortunately**) and social

---

*Which, if you're wondering, is a perfect 0.7.

**Unfortunate for both Gun (for reasons obvious to anyone who has, like myself in a matter of pages, found themselves in the presence of an immensely fuckable member of their favorite gender while contractually and legally obligated to someone else) and the girls in the car (thanks to what is about to happen next, when one man's sin will become another woman's destiny).

standing (rich enough to own two American cars with atrocious track records for reliability, drivability, and resale value and not give a damn, because he can always just buy a new one), all that matters is that he does not look naked or homeless.

What is recorded on both the police report and many media exposés is where they went: I'd never heard of it until of late (because I spent my youth being the kind of conscientious prude middle-aged regrets are built over), but Le Cinq is apparently the biggest nightclub in all of LA. On the outside, it looks like one of those Asian grocery stores my parents and I had to drive across multiple towns for (before H Mart moved in and changed our lives forever), all bright red plastic scaffolding and chrome double doors, stuck in the industrial section of Western Avenue, where Koreatown runs into Wilshire. But on the inside, it resembles Vegas itself, replete with floating LED lights and ceramic gargoyles guarding the bathrooms, perhaps to deter people from having too much sex of the standing-up variety in the stalls. Do not ask me why K-town's hottest nightclub decides to name itself after its business hours, and the wrong ones at that—Le Cinq might mean "five o'clock" in French, but the doors technically do not open until 5:30. Perhaps "Cinq Heures et Demi" is a bit much of a mouthful for the K-town girls and boys whose Engrish was bastardization enough; no need to also try their tongue at Français.

"I hope you've had dinner," is the first thing out of Gun's mouth after Kimme and Ilee tuck their bodies into the back of his two-door Camaro and S is left to fiddle the passenger seat back to its original upright position. It's in surprisingly accent-less English, like the boy's been practicing. From her spot up front, S turns around to look at her comrades—if they haven't been comrades before, they are about to be when the clock strikes twelve—to gauge the best way to respond.

"You are taking us out to dinner," Ilee calls out over the low growl of the V8 engine, also in English, because she has a metaphorical dick that will come in handy both now and later.

"I've already had my il-cha. My wife and I, we ate some, drank more, so she went home early."

"Your wife?" Both S and Ilee say this at the same time, frowning at the layout of Gun's hairline, which has already begun its descent toward the back of his head.

"If you're not married by thirty, everyone thinks there is something fundamentally wrong with you," he says, finally switching back to Korean.

"It is less about true love and more about what the neighbors think?" Ilee rephrases, her Korean following suit.

"Hi, are you Korean?" Gun snorts. "One day in the U.S. and you already forgot how we do things back home?"

"Why come to America, if not to become a little less Korean yourself?" I'm telling you; Ilee is a killer (although alas, not the only one).

"My wife, she is Korean-American, a physicist, you've heard of JPL?" Two can apparently piss in the same contest (just ask my husband and me*).

"We're idols, Korean ones. I've never heard of it. What's JPL?" Kimme breaks in.

"You may have spent your best years in a training camp, but surely you know what NASA is. You know Mars?"

"Bruno or the planet?" It is unclear whether she is joking.

"Bruno Mars is Filipino. Do people know that? There may be hope for you girls yet. Asians in America are finally getting noticed."

"Are you getting noticed these days?" S interjects.

"You know, I get recognized more for being an idol, a former one, than any of my recent television screen roles, by Koreans, that is. There are no American fans yet," Gun admits, not without a little sad-

---

*In the race for who can be more reckless and still stay married, there are no prizes, just a bunch of potentially interesting pit stops upon which I could maybe build a wholly different life.

ness in his voice. In the investigation that follows, it will be too easy to assume a man who is willing to tell the truth is also a good man, in possession of other virtues. Think halo effect,* but for personality traits. In this story, as in others, honesty is not the problem.

By now they are in the parking lot of Le Cinq, the valet ready and waiting like a puppy outside Gun's door, so the four of them descend into the gelatinous evening air thick with secondhand smoke and stereo music emanating from S-class Benzs blasting the bass so loud the cigarette particles vibrate a little in midair. In a week, Ilee will write a song lyric about this moment that discloses both these physical facts about the scene and what happens after, but a libel lawsuit will effectively erase this music from collective memory, except of course for those whose lives remain defined by it.

Gun walks toward the entrance, where yes, there's a metal detector. S glances at Kimme, who looks unfazed, while Ilee looks around, apparently for an exit strategy.

"This isn't LAX, ladies," calls out the only guy they will meet all night who is in a three-piece suit, shiny and ridiculous like something from an earlier, more decadent decade. The manager maybe. The four may not be leaving on a jet plane, but they're going someplace.

This is a full half decade before what happens at Pulse Nightclub turns "Latin Night" to the worst slaying of Americans since 9/11 (only to be outdone a year later by what happens from a Mandalay Bay hotel window in Las Vegas). But Korean-Americans remember April 29, 1992, when police brutality was something twelve jurors deliberated but did not believe in, despite the nationwide broadcast of the graphic evidence over what happened to Rodney King, and three hours later, South Central and its K-town went up in flames as punishment or self-flagellation or the logical next step when social contracts are broken.

---

*See Chapters 4 and 7.

Now, when these girls hover below the cold frame of the metal detector, they chalk it up to America being the unpredictably violent place the rest of the world thinks it is, where a man can buy a gun at the same discount store he purchases his candy or toiletries.

Once inside, S and Ilee look appeased: there is something comforting about the blanket of nicotine and tar dousing the scene with a soft, blurry look normally achieved only by camera filter, the naked pink hot dogs sliced and sitting lazily on plates like stray but harmless dicks without a cause, the ultraviolet bottles of whisky glowing purple under the LED lights like crown jewels. A waiter is talking to Gun. The two men walk toward a booth the shape of the moon and stacked with the standard fare for the night, which is apparently the Hooters menu paired with a cameo from the farmer's market: chicken fingers and seasonal fruits, sliced and assembled into a color wheel. A bottle of Rémy Martin, already poured into four shot glasses, takes the place of a centerpiece.

"Drink first, dance first," says Gun, a non sequitur if there ever is one.

"Where's the bathroom?" asks Ilee.

"Already?" he replies. He doesn't answer her question, only raises one glass and waits patiently for the girls to follow, first S, then Kimme, until the ignored poet finally gives in to peer pressure and tips hers toward the invisible midpoint in the air that they all appear to be saluting. To everyone's surprise, S finishes her potion in one flip of the wrist; it is gone by the time Gun brings his to his lips. He puts his cup down and pours her another. If you are tempted to judge her now, wait.

"I thought they weeded out the alcoholics during training," Gun observes.

"You must be a lightweight," S retorts.

"I've never seen you drink like that," Ilee says.

"We can't drink on camera, and our producer always looks a little constipated when we try to drink anything around him, even beer."

"I will still judge you," Ilee reminds her.

S squints at her friend. "But you'll forgive me after," she predicts.

"Americans have this saying; you've ever heard it? Easier to ask for forgiveness than permission." Gun tips back his own drink before offering this social commentary.

"Does that work with your wife?" S inquires.

He smiles. The answer must be yes.

"I'm going to the bathroom," Kimme announces, unoriginal. As she walks away from the table, her two ass cheeks rotate on the axis of her pelvic bone like gears meant to set men into motion.

"Did the producer give you all laxatives or something?"

Ilee says, "Aloe vera juice. Good for skin but it has laxative effects, did you know? Also, tastes like old bath water, or a chlorine pool that's been sitting out in the sun all day."

"Aloe vera isn't the only thing that tastes like bleach," S agrees. "Although if you drink it enough, other things will start to taste better." She looks at Gun to see if he gets the reference, if he knows that most men are unique in their particular brand of misogyny but all men are the same in the way they taste, chlorine-like and thick. Dudes may not be created equal, but spunk is.

Gun isn't listening.

Pinocchio—when he finds out what happens next—well, even the God of the heaven and earth could not save his only begotten child from public opinion, whose courts, it turns out, are big fans of crucifixion. Do you need me to tell you that two millennia later, not much has changed?

7

The Invisible Gorilla (D-6)

Riddle: In the age of Interpol, paparazzi, and Twitter, where can a man hide?

Answer: In plain sight.

At the risk of providing a template for future fugitives, here is how it happens.

First, a little context: There's this well-known experiment professors love to show introductory psych kids halfway through the semester. It's called the Invisible Gorilla.* *Smithsonian Magazine* did a whole feature on it. It did not involve lots of complicated math but did win an Ig Nobel Prize. The premise is simple: a grainy video shows six ethnically ambiguous—but mostly white, if anyone's guessing—kids dressed in the type of boring clothes designed to make the person wearing them invisible: ill-fitting T-shirts in black and white, eighties-style jeans cut to hide both shape and gender. Between them, a basketball, dull and orange, the color of sunshine during a dust storm. The caption tells us nothing, just says "selective

---

*See Simons and Chabris (1999).

attention test," whatever the hell that means. The instructions are simple: count the number of passes between the players in white.

A minute (twelve passes? fourteen?) later, after it's become thoroughly obvious that everyone in the video is indeed white as hell and has never actually played basketball a day in their lives, the professor hits pause and asks: Well, how many passes?

Here's the thing. The professor doesn't give a fuck about the number of passes. Like a prostitute during the month of Lent, she will nod at whatever number people throw at her. What she is waiting for is for someone to disrupt the conversation and ask, "Wait, what about the gorilla?"

If no one does, because this is the singular occasion where a class demo actually works, then she'll smile before posing the question herself: "Did ya see the gorilla?"

Cue the video, because no one believes that an experiment called the Invisible Gorilla would actually involve one. But lo, when the counting stops, everyone can see the impossible: twelve seconds in, a person of indeterminate gender and age walks into the camera's shot in a full-body gorilla suit—black and matted like a forgotten Halloween costume—thumps their chest, and strolls on out.

For the first and maybe only time in the semester, the kiddos are impressed. They learned something new! Or perhaps more precisely, they found proof for what the smart ones suspected and everyone else still doesn't believe: the world is large, it contains multitudes, and we in our humanness get very little.

Knowing this, try not to disbelieve me when I say that I do not see the eldest member of The Band meandering the frozen foods section of H Mart on one of those usual midweek afternoons when it's two hours post-lunch and the Pacific Coast Highway is already jammed with drivers looking for a reason to be alive. Me, I'm looking for tteokbokki to coat in cornstarch and smother in gochujang and honey, Korean fast food at its best or worst, depending on what the goal is (deliciousness or a long and healthy life). There are the cheapo plain ones tightly packed and stuck together in clear cellophane packaging, looking like a multitude of very short, very pasty fingers. There are the prepackaged ones in pretty boxes, already marinating in stew and promising minimum effort for maximum joy: photos of the rice cakes slathered in red sauce, waiting patiently to be eaten in rustic white bowls, flanked on each side by garnishes and side dishes (hard-boiled eggs, sliced cheese, scallions) deceptively absent from the containers themselves.

"Oryosseul ttae uri ommaga mani han yorieyo,"* says a voice from behind.

I turn. It's unclear whether the boy standing a forearm's distance away is talking to me or himself or, who knows, maybe he's on the phone—a hoodie shrouds his ears, where an earpiece could be hiding.

He laughs and says, "Geunde geunyoneun yorihaji mot haessoyo."**

"Sorry?" I say. Only then does he glance at me. He bows a little, backing away a half foot.

"I'm not actually Korean," I explain, a little embarrassed to be one kind of Asian but shopping in a different Asian's grocery store.

"Ah." He nods vigorously, but then shakes his head, as if changing his opinion on the matter of my ethnic identity.

"Don't worry, I get mistaken for Korean all the time," I tell him. In fifth grade, Ji-Hyun, whom all the teachers called Jenny and all the white kids called (inexplicably) Baby J, was the most popular Korean girl and only deigned to speak to me approximately once a semester.

"Hajimaaa," she quipped during lunch one spring day. When I only looked stupidly in her direction, she stared back for a moment before her hand flew over her mouth. "Oops, I thought you were Korean," she said, apologetic. It was the nicest thing she said to me that

---

*Here's what he really said: 어렸을 때 우리 엄마가 많이 한 요리예요.

**And then: 근데 그녀는 요리하지 못 했어요.

year. Although she immediately switched to English after that, the content itself of what she wanted to say to me only seemed to deteriorate. "Why're you wearing your shirt off your shoulder like that?" she demanded, pulling her own Bebe tee down one skinny arm to expose a glassy knob of skin. "You trying to be sexy or something?" It was most definitely an accusation.

"It's an off-the-shoulder top, duh," I retorted, refusing to be slut-shamed at ten. To which she responded (also inexplicably), squinting, "You mad-dogging me or something?"

I said, "Why do you always say 'or something' at the end of all your sentences?"

She replied, "Wanna take this outside some*time*?"

I didn't remind her that we were already outside, Asian-squatting over the lunch benches to avoid sitting on pigeon poop, and only shook my head. It worked; she only kicked me politely in the shins periodically after that but never challenged me to another duel, which, let's be honest, no one would've died from, but plenty of hair might've been left on the playground after.

"My modder," the boy says. "She make this." He pointed a long, lovely digit at the plastic in my hand, the tip of his index finger curved supernaturally like the neck of a swan. "Her tteokbokki, ah. Not so good," he adds, giggling but then bringing his finger to his lips. "Shh. You no tell her, okay?"

"Okay," I tell him, agreeing even though the premise is entirely wrong; I'd never meet his mother.

His gaze leaves the rice cakes I'm cradling and meanders north, past collarbone and neck, in search of a face to land on. "You Chinese?"

"Yup," I reply. "Sorry." What is it with the ability of certain people to make everybody around them feel sorry that they can not be all things at all times, or at least whenever the person wants? Maybe that is the definition of worship, or charisma: the capacity to make a stranger wish she could be whatever you desire her to be.

"You look Korean," he points out.

"I've been told." After Ji-Hyun came a long stretch devoid of Koreans until Andrew Kim showed up freshman year of college during a Halloween party gone south wherein no one got the memo about not being a racist beforehand. So a good half of the white people showed up in varying colors of face—black, brown, red, yellow. A blonde chick as Flavor Flav, replete with plastic gold chains and a grill to match, came bearing six-packs and brownies with a heavily contoured Pocahontas, weirdly reminiscent of Kim K. A spray-tanned Australian couple arrived empty-handed as Aladdin and Jasmine, if Aladdin had a slight beer gut and Jasmine let herself go a little bit so as to not make her lover feel too bad about himself. Then there were the two redheads in boxy kimonos and a third in the world's most revelatory cheongsam, slit up to labia majora and so much spandex that everyone at the party could draw her belly button with forensic precision if asked.

Andrew saw me in my Sailor Moon outfit from across the room, my two pigtails thick and lopsided, brown booty shorts up to the ungodly place where ass meets thigh, counteracted only by the presence of a pair of old nylons underneath, stolen from my mother—in other words, a terrible and shameless costume made miraculously better by the fact that unlike the gringos in the room, I was the same ethnicity as the character I was impersonating. Or close enough, at least, China being one extended armada away from Japan. Andrew trekked over and did not explain his own outfit—an ill-fitting durag that bore an uncanny resemblance to my own black pantyhose, with a Snickers bar in hand—or introduce himself before laying an arm across my back. "We need to leave now," he said, surveying the room.

When I did nothing, only stared at him curiously, he let out a little sigh. "Before someone takes a photo of these people's costumes and we are guilty by association." He let go of my back and latched on to a hand instead; with a little tug, I couldn't help but follow him across the room and down the crooked stairs.

"What are you dressed up as?" I demanded when we finally stopped outside on the street, in lieu of "thanks" or "hello, who are you again?"

"Ima candy (w)rapper," he said, stone-faced. "Get it?"

It took me a second, but then a follow-up: "You're allowed to dress up as a Black person but white folks aren't allowed to dress up as Asians?"

Andrew only shrugged, undeterred, maybe because he had been called many things in his life by many people—"chink" by the Hispanic kids at Victor Elementary, back when people still referred to them as Hispanic; "four-eyes" by the uninspired bullies at Bert Lynn Middle School, before his parents gave in and bought him contacts; "lady-beater" by his girlfriend at West High, when she found out that he had, on occasion, hit his mother—but "racist" was never one of them, and he considered himself immune.

"Who says I'm dressed up as a Black rapper? Asians can rap too." It was a prophecy for The Band if there ever was one, though at this precise moment in time, neither of us had met, known, or heard of any Asian rappers. But still, at least one of us believed. He glanced down at me without lingering too long on any particular body part. "You're allowed to dress up as Sailor Moon even though you aren't Japanese," he countered.

"How'd you know?" I inquired, a little surprised that we did not all look the same, even to each other.

"I'm Korean," he said. Then, "You're either Korean or Chinese," staring at the center of my face until I was forced to look away, a little embarrassed by the scrutiny.

"I'm Chinese," I told him.

"That's too bad," he replied, letting go of my hand finally. "I suppose it was too good to be true." Before I could ask what he was referring to, he added, "We can just be friends, then, I guess."

Andrew kept his promise: he never touched me again after that first meeting, despite all my subsequent efforts to woo him by picking up his native tongue from a pair of Rosetta Stone CDs. He only stared at my mouth intently every time we went out for kimchi and KFC (of the Korean, not Kentucky, variety) before letting his eyes wander farther south, toward another pair of lips. I wondered but did not ask if Korean men might naturally appreciate the taste of pussy more because they spent their whole lives eating the kind of fermented foods whose trademark tang was such an acquired taste. Instead I practiced my Hangul while we discussed the incomprehensible things in our lives:

roommates who believed clothing to be optional (his);
suitemates who considered cordless landline phones to double as a dildo when not in use (mine);
cell phone minutes that were free on nights and weekends but whose definition of "night" (seven p.m.? midnight?) and "weekend" (did Friday count?) never could be pinned down (both of ours);
double meanings behind our friends' AOL screen names ("callmetherapist" = "call me therapist" or "call me the rapist?")

Our flirtation survived a subsequent trio of my nonexclusive flings with lesser men and his protracted monogamy with a graduate student instructor from his department. It prevailed through his shame-inducing confession about still (occasionally) hitting his own mother and my stress-induced bout with cystic acne. Sometime during the prolonged purgatory period between graduating college and becoming a fully functional adult, it descended into hibernation when he became a pastor and I, in a retributive fury, became the type of woman he now has to pray for—if or when he thinks of me at all, which, Lord willing, is (almost) never. I, too, might've forgotten about it forever had it not been for what is about to happen next.

The boy introduces himself first. "Duri," he says.

"What's that?" I ask. Curiously, all the Koreans I've known up to this point since Andrew have either Americanized names almost exclusively from the Bible (Daniel, David, John, Peter, Paul, Hannah, Esther, Grace, Eunice) or else a handful of prototypical hyphenated ones from their native tongue (Ji-, Hye-). But maybe that is part of the American experiment of being an immigrant: blending in as much as possible with either each other or fellow Americans so as to rouse the minimal amount of suspicion possible and avoid being noticed by the powers that be, who, based on both historical data and recent observation, have a bad habit of coming down terrifyingly, fatally hard on other minority groups without the "model" in front of their name.

"Duri," he repeats, yanking down his hoodie to reveal a canvas of bangs, neatly circumscribing the entirety of his head like an inky ceramic bowl. His face looks familiar, but it's not obvious to me yet whether it's familiar the way all attractive people are familiar in their embodiment of the species' Platonic ideal, or familiar in the much more particular way of having been seen before. His left eye is almost imperceptibly larger than the right, but rather than this being a nick against his otherwise symmetrical features, it gives him a gamely quality, one that makes him look slightly amused, or at least ready for come what may as long as it has the potential to end in amusement. "Duri, my name."

"Duri, like the fruit?" (In high school, the smart Asians referred to me as the "Asian blonde"; a person doesn't have to search too far to find the reason.) "You know, durian?" On my phone, I find a picture of the redolent monster fruit, its fleshy yellow insides protruding pornographically from its spiky encasement like a womb, or a boner.

"Durian!" he cries, hiccupping a little with a laugh that bubbles before it pops. I imagine it is the first time he's been insulted by a stranger via comparison with the world's stinkiest and ugliest plant species. "I'm more pretty," he insists. "I'm Pretty Boy."

This moniker triggers the obvious: Duh! Pretty Boy is what the fandom calls the oldest and most conventionally attractive member of The Band. "The Visual" may be an industry term, but Pretty Boy is a term of endearment bestowed by those who love him the most aggressively, made all the more popular since their global takeover and acquisition of international followers who will say his real name in every possible pronunciation (sang, soong, seng, see-yong) except the correct one (sung du-ri). In that sense, Pretty Boy is as much of a nickname as a bone to everyone involved, saving him from hearing his own name butchered ad infinitum by exceedingly confident but linguistically stunted Americans, and saving said fans from having to try too hard and learn something new. Plus, it fits. His base is known to post entire manifestos online, counting the precise ways that this man is more pretty than beautiful or cute or handsome. Beauty is too damn subjective, and cuteness implies a youth he does not possess, and handsomeness involves a necessary level of testosterone that in the present cultural climate is treated as a liability more than anything else. Pretty is the perfect palate pleaser; pretty is the platonic ideal. Everyone loves pretty, just like everybody loves Duri, until they realize that loving someone also means that you can expect things from them and judge them when they deviate from the brunt force of those expectations. If the opposite of hate is not love but indifference, then love must involve giving a lot of shits, endless shits, really, and when it's just one person or a few people who love you, it's one thing. It's doable, tolerable, precious even, enough to build whole institutions (marriage) and civilizations (family) around. When it's a couple of millions of strangers who know you only by your reflection, then love is less of a feeling and more of a tsunami, one that is almost impossible to survive without drowning.

The tteokbokki is dripping, already thawing in my hand. The boy—Duri—notices and says, "You know how to make it?" He looks skeptical.

"I panfry them in a little oil, then dip them in hot sauce and honey," I offer.

"No no no. Wrong way. You—" He motions at something circular and heavy.

"A pot instead? I should be using a pot?" I ask. "Deep-fry, not panfry?"

More head-shaking from him, followed by an up-and-down motion with one hand. It's unclear whether he's demonstrating some advanced cooking technique or simulating a blow job. I'd offer him one right there in the frozen food aisle if only Rosetta Stone had bypassed all the useless nouns in the beginner's section (dog, pencil, school, child) and instead told me what I really wanted to know (namely, how to curse or proposition persons of interest).

"Aach," he said finally, dropping his hands. "I teach you."

"You teach me where?" It is my turn to be the skeptic. It is true that men have spent my whole life offering to teach me things. Dad's pedagogical style involved gifting me, every middle school summer, a different college textbook in each of the physical sciences and an IKEA desk in its original packaging to assemble myself so as to have a place to pursue said summer reading. High school teachers, if they were elderly and female, frequently accused me of not writing things in my own words whenever I deployed some vocabulary term they themselves did not know (*pollicitation*: a promise that hasn't been accepted; *eupeptic*: having good digestion), but if they were young and male, read my pompous shit aloud to the rest of class and whispered things like "motherfucking genius right there" and "come see me after class." College professors, who unanimously lectured well but were allergic to other forms of instruction, opted to hand me off to their teaching assistants, who told me everything I needed to know for the exams and nothing I needed to know for making sense of it in life. Graduate school mentors dosed out advising sessions that, when taken as prescribed once a week, promised to fend off any pressing desires to either kill myself or die trying. Most recently, hubby taught me to live properly by teaching me the following, in no particular order: the secrets to both real estate (location, location, location) and good head (saliva, saliva, saliva; also, two hands), the trick to getting a marriage proposal (being a virgin beforehand, or at least insisting that you are, and when you find yourself suddenly not one, crying really hard while whispering, "Am I still a virgin?" even though you know full well the answer to that), and the strategy for keeping a man interested after a decade of being inside the same vagina every weekend (an ongoing supply of potential replacement men, some imaginary and some real).

Upon further reflection, even my own current students, the boys, at least, find mansplaining an almost irresistible temptation: the side of town the best street tacos be at (the shitty side, for a long list of sociological reasons), the appropriate amount of time needed to recover from a non-mutual breakup (twenty-nine days; anything past a month implies a desperation that no one finds appealing, not even fellow desperados), and the reason that *The Sopranos* remains the best show in television history (something about an antihero who managed to be old, fat, psychopathic, and immensely fuckable). The cumulative evidence thus far suggests that I shouldn't be surprised when another man enters my life stage left, ready to teach me a thing or two.

"You have house?" he inquires.

"Yes?" When fact proves more bizarre than fiction, it is difficult not to say the most factual of statements as a question.

"Okay, I follow you," he replies.

I don't understand what he's saying or even implying, but I can't help but be immensely trusting of the dependability of attractive strangers to guarantee that nothing bad will happen. See also:

Halo effect: The tendency to assume that physically attractive people, because they have the one good trait we can see, possess all the other good traits: kindness, understanding, safety, mental stability. Need I tell you that this is a lie?

At checkout, the cashier scans our dual packs of macerating tteokbokki without looking up. Based on a speedy and fairly prejudicial survey of her age and ethnic origins, I say it's unlikely she noticed Duri and recognized him as the Pretty Boy. There are few types of people as uninterested in celebrity as elderly Asian women who have seen too much in their own lives—foreign occupations, cultural revolutions, bad husbands—to be bothered by the extenuating circumstances of other people, particularly anyone they don't call son.

"Gidariseyo,"* he says. "Waiting, waiting." Scooting backward, he descends back into the belly of the store that is lined with rows as tight as teeth. The cashier is my only chance of finding an interpreter, but she is busy spraying the conveyer belt with a fine mist of pink toxins that smell of hospital, then scrubbing furiously with an excessive wad of paper towels—three or four whole sheets in a row, an extravagance I've never seen any Asian person employ with a paper product they paid for themselves.

Seconds, minutes—would anyone believe me if I said it felt like days?—before Duri comes back bearing dried anchovies and kelp in matching cellophane wrapping, one silvery and ghastly, a thousand tiny fish bodies compressed inside an incongruously decorative emerald box, the other brown and dull, like skin without a body. Under one armpit, he has a noisy packet of fish cakes, round and wrinkly and bearing an unappetizing resemblance to old testicles; under the other, three stalks of scallions rubber-banded together and a precarious carton of eggs.

"Sorry, sorry," he says, a bone thrown to no particular person but free for the taking for either of the women in his presence, whoever has more irritation to burn. He digs into his pants, extracting a graf-

*According to Papago, this is what he really said: 기다리세요

fitied wallet with a giant 두 scratched into the pebbled leather on one side, desecrating the embossed logo of Chanel's interlocking Cs, and 리 into the other, like a kindergarten craft project gone terribly wrong, but in his case, probably just the byproduct of an extended afternoon in an airport VIP lounge with spotty internet and nothing on TV.

"I've got money," I tell him.

He makes no indication of having heard. Perhaps his English is that bad. More likely, he is just showing off the uniquely male skill of not hearing a woman whenever she says something of no consequence. The black card in his hand glows softly like the volcanic sand beaches of some exotic island. Were it not for its telltale chip centered on the far end, I would not know it's a credit card it all, so minimalist is the information that it contains: no financial institution listed, not even the ubiquitous duo of overlapping red and yellow circles (Mastercard) or clunky white block letters (VISA) topped with an excessive string of numbers, spaced apart in groups of four like a bad set of dentures. In lieu of any Arabic numerals to identify a man and his lot, there are hieroglyphics, an octet of symbols resembling the Wingdings I knew as a child of Microsoft and the nineties: ✳ ⚱ ✝ ☞ ✚? Typography is not my forte; I don't read dingbat. Luckily, my illiteracy doesn't matter. The little black card reader on the counter appears to understand exactly what it says. It doesn't ask for a tap or a signature. Maybe that's what wealth really buys: the ability to be left alone and unbothered by the million bits of unnecessary efforts expended that the rest of us have to get through just to make it home alive.

In the parking lot facing the Pacific Coast Highway, I glance at Duri, but he is already walking away. I'm less concerned about what is supposed to happen next and more interested in making it home with my own pack of tteokbokki, which he is carrying in the singular milky bag the cashier gave us.

"So—"

"I follow you," he shouts, because he has to; he's that far away—which is good, because my car is less of a vehicle and more of a repository for things the men in my life do not care enough about to keep track of.* Worn socks, tucked into themselves from recent wear, and shorn jackets hide what lurks below: encrusted mugs, Tupperware, wrappers, golf tees, coins, magnets, Hot Wheels, last week's mail, Thomas the Train and his extended family of steamies, coins, straws, Bibles, picture books. Once I found a whole burrito, uneaten and still wrapped, in the no-man's-land between the passenger seat and console; it explained the heady, ripe smell of carcass meets old dairy that had been invading the car for days.

Another time, many years ago, I found a spoon, a fancy silver one, whose stem was engraved with the kind of swirls and whorls that I imagine, rightly or wrongly, a certain class of WASP woman likes—the kind of woman whose idea of literary fiction is Jane Austen and who will find a man more sexually appealing if he speaks with a British accent. This discovery led to the firm conviction that my husband was having an affair with a mousy white woman we had both met at the park—Maureen was her name—who fit that precise criteria. He denied it, calling me a lunatic. I demanded a more rational explanation for the presence of a spoon that I did not own and would never purchase or gift. He couldn't provide one, only shrugged, unbothered by the existence of silverware whose ancestry could not be traced. I kept the spoon for forensic evidence in case I would ever need to prove myself as a woman wronged, but over the years and after the onboarding of many children (anything over one child is "many," or so it feels), I can no longer tell you where that fucking spoon is. I continue to keep an eye on the debris left behind in the car, defying

---

*Studies show: men and women register a mess equally well, but the gender difference is this—men feel no urgency about the matter, whereas women feel compelled to do something about it (see: Thébaud et al. 2021).

scientists by neglecting to clean up, although here it is less about gender equality and more about being right about the spoon, the original sin that spawned the others, including the ones to come.

PCH is already a parking lot, littered with drivers alternating between aggressive maneuvering to surpass other drivers and idling on their phone whenever their efforts prove worthless. It's a miracle that in my rearview mirror, I can see Duri's characteristic onyx hood and sweep of bangs, his trademark curved fingers dangling out the window of his rental, the kind of monstrous black car usually reserved for dictators and drug lords, all height and grill and tinted glass. He is a surprisingly good driver, calm and adept and able to stay inside the lines (whether my surprise comes from his Asianness or young maleness or celebrity status as someone who always has a chauffeur—take your guess). We crawl up the Hill, following Hawthorne Boulevard until the clumps of strip malls and chain restaurants and major retailers disappear. With each additional city block of incline, another one of their kind gets eliminated, and only lengthy streets well-endowed with trees remain, as if we were in a video game (*Grand Theft Auto V*) wherein the highest level involves transcending the urbanity of Los Santos to arrive at the sprawling nature of Mt. Chiliad.

When we pull into the extensively groomed village of matchy-matchy McMansions of Wallace Ranch—which give them the unfortunate quality of looking like a plaza of town houses—my question is this: Should I have warned the parties involved? My general policy with both strangers and husbands has always been a practice I borrowed from the military à la the Clinton administration (don't ask, don't tell), but for both Bill and myself, it's unclear how well it's been working. Perhaps I should've warned Luc I was bringing home a boy I found at the store. Maybe I should've also told the boy that my house comes with a husband and two poorly trained pets I refer to as children. I should probably think about my actions more before committing to them.

Duri parks noiselessly behind me, the back end of his Land Rover sticking unscrupulously into the street, then follows me through the garage to the kitchen with such a lack of ceremony that I wonder if in a past life he's lived here before and therefore knows the layout.

"Cozy," he says.

"Thank you," I say, even though it's an insult. Nobody pays for cozy. *Cozy* is reserved for real estate agents in need of a euphemism for *small*. "But you know, there's five bedrooms." I'm not a petty person, but I'm not Jesus either. I need validation as much as the next mortal.

"Wow," he replies, already losing interest and in search of better things in the fridge. "Gochujang," he says, squinting at the lit insides brimming with yesterday's leftovers and last week's plans. "Where?"

It's hiding on the refrigerator door under a landfill of ketchup packets and single servings of crushed red pepper flakes, scaffolded by its spicier relatives: sriracha, harissa, 老干妈/Lao Gan Ma sauce—a brotherhood of condiment from both the Middle and Far East. I hand it to him, but he's counting out the number of red pepper packets instead. Are we playing a game of *If You Give a Mouse a Cookie*? I must be caught in the crossfire of a Korean version of *Punk'd* or *Candid Camera* or some other reality TV show where schadenfreude is the whole point of the game, or its close cousin: joy at not your enemy's suffering, but delight at the bewilderment of strangers for the viewing pleasure of still other strangers. Or maybe this is a new spin-off of *Undercover Boss* but it's celebrities going in plain sight to demonstrate just how far a grown woman, mother of two and wife of one, will immolate herself to the whims of somebody who calls himself the Pretty Boy. The Pretty Boy! And you thought all Asians were smart. Or women were less shallow than men.

Luc enters stage left from the garage, with Sam and Kilim behind. Kilim isn't a homonym for "kill 'em"; it's short for Kilimanjaro. Before I get questioned on why I named my second-born after an active volcano in Tanzania despite being neither African nor a climber nor even a fan of any outdoor activity, really, consider my alternatives. I wasn't going to name him after the NFL's most middle-aged quarterback ("Brady," a contender on the popularity charts for America's top boy names since 1883, with peak success around 2007–2008, when Tom Brady was on a dry spell between Super Bowl rings number three and four) or New York's dirtiest river ("Hudson," which no one named their kid ever for the entirety of the twentieth century until just before the millennium, when it started appearing on birth certificates across not just New York but the other forty-nine inferior states as well). As for other, more familiar choices surging across OB wards, I had no interest in calling out my son's name in a playground and having three kids come running. I hate all children except my own. Remember that, when you invariably start questioning my other life choices.

"Hey?" It's a question, not a greeting, from Luc's mouth. His eyes dart from Duri, who is now meticulously dumping the red pepper flakes into a countertop bowl, to me, standing stupidly in my own kitchen with no explanation to grasp at.

Duri, upon hearing the voice of another male in the room, immediately looks up and then ducks his head down again for a little bow, not deep enough to make the white man feel awkward but not imperceptible to the other Asian in the room. "How do you do, nice to meet you," he declares. Then, "Husband?"

"For the time being," says Luc, just as I quip, "My first one, yes." Luc, of course, takes my joke as a sign that he can speak freely. "You know, I know I've said that I've always wanted to come home and find you deep diving into some other man's lap, looking for lost treasure, but this"—his fingers make a little twirl in the air, like he's trying to lasso some invisible horse—"isn't exactly what I had in mind. I figured the two of you would be doing something more interesting than whatever the hell this is."

"Shut up," I tell him, unsure of whether a joke that's repeated more than once is both no longer funny and not a joke. But what I'm really wondering is how much English Duri actually speaks. He can apparently read my mind even if he can't comprehend my words, so he says, "Sorry, no English."

Sam, who at this point has been inching silently across the oak floor with the wary look of a fifth grader used to his parents' incomprehensible banter, asks, "Can I go play my Xbox—"

"Yes," Luc cuts him off. "I don't want to see you until dinner."

Kilim, at three, appears to just now register the presence of a new human in his home. He holds up a flashy die-cast vehicle the colors of Halloween in Duri's direction and asks, "Want to see my new Hot Wheels car?"

Duri walks over to and gives him a little pat on the head. "Handsome!" he says, after a moment of evaluation: the gray eyes, hair the color of milk poured into tea, opaque skin. "Hangugeso geuron aedeul omchong joahaeyo,"* he adds.

"You speak Korean now?" Luc asks me.

"I spent the pandemic diddling around on Duolingo after we couldn't agree on any more Netflix shows to watch after *The Tiger King*, remember? But no, my Korean has not noticeably improved. Other than *annyeonghaseyo* and *ne*, all I remember are the Korean words that sound just like the Chinese ones. Like *dong wu* and *dongmul*." I try to think harder, but it's no use: I forget about *pibu* (*pífū*), *dong-ui* (*tóngyì*), *yong-gi* (*yǒngqì*), *jeonbu* (*quánbù*). Skin, agree, courage, everything. These I will remember later, when it'll be necessary to use them in conversation.

"Hello, yes, animal," says Duri, translating, arms wrist deep in a mixing bowl full of water, brimming with rehydrated anchovy and seaweed.

---

*한국에서 그런 애들 엄청 좋아해요

"What'd he just say?" demands Luc, even though it's clear from his tone that he heard perfectly well and is responding accordingly. "Did he just say to you, 'Yes, animal'?" A pause. "I didn't know the two of you had that kind of relationship already." Turning to the guest: "What's your name again?"

"I'm Pretty Boy," says Duri. Is that a smirk?

"You've got to be fucking kidding me." Luc says this like an accusation. He looks around in search of someone to hand it to.

"Fucking A!" shouts Kilim between car noises (*vruum, tuck, ah-ooga*).

"Jjeut-jjeut,"* says Duri, looking down from the scallions he's now slicing to glance at the small child making figure eights around his flocked feet. "Bad word!" American profanity must be one of our most exported goods, recognized the world over.

"Where'd you find this guy?" The tines between Luc's eyebrows deepen.

"We met at H Mart just now. He's gonna show me how to make rice cakes the proper way."

"Is this what you do when I'm not around?"

"Apparently it's what I do when you *are* around. Luc, Duri. Duri, Luc."

"Hello, Luc," Duri says obediently.

"You and my mother." From Luc's mouth, this, too, is an accusation. "You two are the same person."

"She has a soft spot for Asian men?" But then: "That can't be right, because all four of your mother's husbands are white."

"What I mean is, she also believes in bringing home random men she finds off the street. Steph—the last husband—was one of those. She always told my dad they met at a protest. She neglected to mention the fact that she was the one protesting, and he just happened to be wandering around Occidental campus because that was basically his living room, seeing that he was homeless."

---

*쯧쯧. Tsk-tsk.

"Was Steph the alcoholic or the wife-beater? I get her third and fourth husbands confused."

"It's C, both of the above. Apparently homelessness, alcoholism, and bad impulse control go together."

"That's what we call domestic violence now? Bad impulse control?"

"You know what else we call bad impulse control? Bringing home random men from the store."

"You know The Band?" Duri interrupts.

Luc squints. "The Korean one?" There was only one musical act who had dared to call themselves that, and the entitlement paid off. Prophecies were almost always self-fulfilling for those who believe.

"You know it," Duri replies, idiomatic and rather smug.

"You two share the same taste in music?" Luc inquires.

"Me, I am in The Band."

At this, Luc squints again, as if he could recognize Korean idols by sight or had the slightest idea what any of them looked like in particular or could bypass outgroup homogeneity effects in general.

Outgroup homogeneity: the tendency to perceive all members of a group that you don't belong to as looking the same. See: alllooksame.com. See also: confusing Lawrence Fishburne with Samuel L. Jackson.

"You are pretty good-looking," he admits.

"I'm Pretty Boy," Duri reminds him.

"Fine," Luc says. "But don't get any ideas," he adds over his shoulder, walking away in search of other rooms of the house where there are no domestic activities like cooking and only rich, manly silence or the kind of static, undemanding sound coming from lovely devices that behave themselves and not beloved people who (fortunately or unfortunately?) do not. Kilim stays behind, still stuck to the floor, where all his toys reside, quietly mumbling some midcentury Chinese song that his grandmother taught him about little girls dropping their handkerchiefs.

Duri looks up and says, "You have pot?"

"For cooking? Unless you're talking about weed. You know—" I show, not tell, pinching my fingers together before bringing them to my lips and sucking in. Having never smoked a thing in my life—not even cigarettes—this is an approximation. I have no idea what smoking cannabis looks like, and by the looks of it, Duri doesn't either; he appears resigned to my overall uselessness and starts perusing the cabinets himself before extracting a heavy Le Creuset number the color of Caribbean seas, turquoise with a hint of ombre—nothing like the stark blue-gray oceans where Palos Verdes and San Pedro meet.

He fills the Dutch oven with water, then adds the fish and kelp. Before it starts to approximate an aquarium too much, he dumps in the hot pepper flakes, chopped scallions, and a dollop of gochujang. He closes the lid, and we glance at each other like strangers in an elevator, unsure of whether to speak or wait quietly for the other person to leave.

"Why are you here?" Despite my cultural and gender group memberships, I have the occasional gift of being able to say aloud what everyone else is thinking.

Duri points to the thawed tteokbokki and anthropomorphic fish cakes waiting patiently for the stock to boil, both still stuck inside their original packaging.

"Where's The Band?" I'm not part of the official fandom—I'm too self-absorbed to be devoted to anything that didn't come out of my own entrails (just ask my husband)—but the whole world, including those who had never heard of them before (like Luc), saw them win their first Grammy just two months prior, for Album of the Year no less. On the gilded stage, the quintet looked like exotic royalty in their jewel-toned Alexander McQueen, all leather and tweed in hues not even fashion editors had seen leather and tweed in before. Who knew cow and sheep could be dyed those colors? Cerise paired with indigo and celadon mix-matched with vermilion, a veritable crown of gems for everyone's viewing pleasure.

Min cried a little, causing him to hand over the mic to the maknae line—the three youngest—who took turns thanking Yesu, their umma, and Justin Bieber, respectively, for reasons that remain foggy given how little Jesus, their mothers, and the American boy wonder had to do with the win. The Genius of Gwangju took this opportunity to announce their next album—they don't call him the Smart One for nothing—to be released this month, while Yoojin chimed in with a long list of producers, collaborators, cowriters, and staff he must've memorized since their debut for such a moment as this. Only Duri said nothing, just blinked and rubbed his eyes, like Saul on the road to Damascus or the blind man at Bethsaida—all men on the verge of some great transformation, an unveiling of sorts, an issue of manifest destiny. The drama with the music video for his birthday single happened after, in a matter of weeks, as soon as the buzz from that historic night wore off and everyone found themselves on the same hedonic treadmills as before. Then, of course, the sudden exit—disappearance, if you will, according to the people whose own lives hinged on the lives of the more interesting people they followed—until he emerged (submerged?) here, now, in front of an overpriced French pot, making a potentially underwhelming dinner.

"Ack—eh." I'm unsure if this is supposed to be Korean or just some sound, the universal noise for a shrug. Then: "Papago," he says into his phone. Behold, magic: Duri mumbles into his Android, lips almost touching his screen, and his phone unravels his words into their English counterparts, its voice cold and metallic but clear as day. This is what it says:

"I think you figured out who I am, otherwise you would not have let me follow you home without asking any questions. Unless Americans are all this trusting. But I don't think so. See, I know who you are too—"

"I'm not anybody," I tell him.

"—everybody in my life is a somebody. If they are not famous, then they are important. They shoot our videos or choreograph our dances or do our makeup, they are on the company payroll and directory and can be looked up or found and they have an interest in The Band. But you look like you could be a nobody—"

I suspect it is a uniquely female condition to be utterly offended but still be propelled by some ancient and patriarchal desire to listen and please the other person, especially if they're male, particularly if they have a minimum of one redeeming physical quality—a wingspan you could yoke oxen to, a face you could break a fall with.

Or maybe it is just me and my terrible, no good, very bad womanism talking.

"Wait," I interrupt. "You could've talked all along with that app translating everything for you?" This appears to me like the more important question. But the boy is on a roll, or maybe apps, like humans, are very bad at multitasking and can't translate my English into Korean at the same time it is using all its core processing power to spin his first language to my second. Regardless, the parties involved bypass the question and continue:

"If you were a fan, this would be out of the question, too much, too much something, that I am sure. But you asked me if my name was Durian!" At this, Duri giggles again, a little in disbelief or relief, I can't tell. "Although you recognized the Pretty Boy nickname, I could see it in your face. Yet you acted the same afterward. Did not even ask for a selca or anything, just talked about your terrible cooking technique—"

"I'm not Korean!" I remind him.

"I forgive you; it is okay. I left you at the cashier to see if you were a good person and would wait for me—"

"Wait, that was a trick?"

Either Duri can understand English better than he speaks it or he is a very gifted mind reader, because his phone translates this next: "Test, more like it. Then when you tried to pay for the food even after seeing my Hyundai Black card, that is when I knew I could trust you. Even The Band members let me pay for everything, me being the oldest, even though we all have the same number of shares in the IPO and all own basically the same apartment, just on different floors."

"You plan on going back to them at some point?"

"I like it here for the time being. Your children do not know who I am. And your husband, he does not care about me, you."

"Me *or* you?" I ask. "Or me *and* you?" Sometimes a single conjunction can change everything. Sometimes I need a stranger to tell me things I would never believe coming out of the mouth of anybody I've shared a tax return with. "Which one does my husband not care about?"

Duri puts down his phone and gives me a familiar look, one I've probably handed out myself to middle schoolers who still believe in Santa and to grown-ups who still believe the election was stolen. "Me and you," he diagnoses at last, likely because it seems like the compassionate option. In the rankings for husbands, between "not jealous" and "indifferent" lies a vast chasm of interpretation.

"What exactly would you like to happen next?" I want to know.

Duri lifts the cast-iron lid and peers inside in search of thickening and a break in surface tension.

"Eat me," he says in English.

The question remains: How much English does Duri actually speak?

8

Duri, Duri

Dinner is about as bad as expected. It's not that Duri lacks skill. His knife technique alone suggests a serious person who does not mess around when the lengths of vegetables are at stake. More likely, Duri has never before fed white people, for whom certain genres of Asian cooking tend to be widely accepted and adored: anything involving a grill (Korean BBQ), high heat (stir- or deep-frying, take your pick), dead animals (at least the varieties that can be found in the Old MacDonald song), a soy sauce base (everyone loves umami, even those who can't pronounce it), and/or an abundance of added sugar (sweetness being a pleasure as old as survival). Other types of Eastern cuisine, though, are not so universally beloved: clear broths or dense soups, sea creatures that lack gills or fins (abalone) or are pounded into suspicious shapes, anything too sticky.

Duri and I slurp away at the red stew, breathing heavily to combat the pain from the heat produced by the gochujang and compounded by the pepper flakes, but Kilim and Sam only gnaw listlessly on their formerly frozen corndogs while glancing at us with a skepticism outpaced only by Luc's.

"I'm not racist," Luc declares. "But what the hell is this again?"

"Tteokbokki," Duri offers.

"Rice cakes," I remind my husband. "Also, things that start with 'I'm not racist but' usually end up being precisely that."

Luc looks like he would like to call me a few names that would blow racism out of the water, but then he says, "Don't give me that. I always eat what you put in front of me."

"I alternate between Mexican, Italian, and Midwestern. It's pretty much a weekly rotation between street tacos, pasta, and a casserole featuring whatever remaining cheese I can find at the back of the fridge. Maybe Indian if we're feeling adventurous or Mediterranean if I'm feeling really nice. It's not exactly a stretch most of the time."

Luc stabs a fish ball and holds it up in midair for everyone to see, like a beheaded enemy. "What exactly is this?"

"I thought your general policy is don't ask, don't tell."

"Maybe when it's about what you do when I'm not around"—he glances at Duri as he says this, but Duri has eyes only for the bowl below him—"but this?" He shakes the ball; it neither jiggles nor bounces. "This looks like somebody's missing cojones."

"Cojones?" inquires Duri.

Papago, which apparently, like Alexa and Suri, is also always listening, beats me to it by answering: "Gohwan." The screen lights up with the corresponding ideograph: 고환.

Duri nearly falls over. He's shaking with the kind of laughter that starts in the gut and ends on the floor.

"I didn't know your app could translate Spanish," I tell him.

He ignores me and says to Luc, "You funny guy."

Luc smiles, and finally looks defanged. "I am pretty funny," he agrees, popping said fish cake into his mouth at last, then appearing to swallow without having masticated. "Remember when you used to laugh at my jokes like that, honey?"

"I do," I tell him, a little sad. Two relationships—both mine, one consensual and ludicrous, the other, not so much—changed all that for us.* With two kids, a mortgage, and the rest of middle age staring us down the barrel, severance was too expensive, and we were both too tired to test whether we could make it separately but broke(n). Sometimes the best institutions are the ones a person can't leave; it makes them more precious that way.

Duri stops laughing and peers at the two of us curiously, with an almost anthropological intensity, as if watching two animals mate en plein air. He recovers almost immediately and says, "I have hotel."

"You inviting my wife to go back with you, or is this your way of saying goodbye?"

"No," is his immediate reply. Then, "You have five bedrooms?"

Luc looks at me. "What else did you tell this guy?"

"I pay you instead of hotel," Duri offers.

"Don't be ridiculous," I tell him.

"Is that a no, or are you inviting him to sleep over for free?" Luc asks.

"What about your stuff?" Now it is my turn to do the ignoring. Married men are always more easily ignored than their unhinged counterparts.

"I check out," Duri admits. "Too easy to die by myself." He shudders, and I can see it now: Duri in his ritzy hotel bathroom, all Carrara marble and subway tile, so white and so clean it resembles an atheist's vision of heaven, the kind of sanatorium a person might not be able to leave. He turns on the shower, then changes his mind. He pours himself a bath because why not? For the first time in his adult life, he has the time. But his legs are too long to extend—the dimensions of tubs are made for women, and there is nowhere to lay his sweet head—a problem that makes him inexplicably think of baby Jesus before him, who also found himself torn from the heights of

_____

*See my next novel for the full story.

heaven in order to try his hand slumming it up with mere mortals in a far-off land, a choice that, with the Lord as with our beloved, was easily blamed on their fathers. The bath water is too hot, then too cold. The towels are on the other side of the room, stupidly sitting on a chrome shelf above the toilet. There is nothing to read. He doesn't like books anyway, and magazines are too terrifying because there is always the good possibility he is inside one against his will.

So, dripping, he pads past the arched doorway into the belly of the room—sorry, suite—whose soft, monochromatic linens are no match for the jarring view of the Angeleno skyline standing sentry outside the double-paned windows, all jagged lines and blinking lights made ever so slightly more bearable by the glare-diffusing powers of voile. Is there anything more depressing than an empty hotel bed in an alien country populated by three hundred million strangers, none of whom know that you're there? He looks back at the bathroom and notices the shower rod bolted into the walls like the monkey bars from which he used to hang a lifetime ago. He wonders if they could support his weight now. That's when he knows he's in trouble.

"What are you trying to say?" I demand. I can envision it, clear as rain. Still, there is no way, I think, that he is suggesting what I think he's suggesting. But then again: John Belushi at the Chateau Marmont, Coco Chanel at the Ritz, Anna Nicole Smith at the Hard Rock, Janis Joplin at the Landmark, Whitney Houston at the Beverly Hilton—

"Anthony Bourdain," Luc interjects, because apparently we can now read each other's minds, and that alone may be reason enough to stay together. Being with someone new—that requires too much goddamn learning. "What was the name of that French hotel where he died? Le something. Champagne or Chambray? Chambard?"

"How do you know this?" Another demand from me, but this time it's unclear if I'm interrogating Luc or Duri. Maybe both.

My husband squints at the boy I've brought home, as if eyes could be windows. Duri blinks but then looks away, as unused to the male gaze as any little girl.

"The downstairs office," I tell them both, trying to break their hex. "He can stay in there. It's got a bed and a computer."

"I have computer," our guest says. "I have everything."

Come to find out, he isn't kidding.

While Luc is out searching for a burrito to compensate for his unfinished stew still steeping on the dinner table, Duri goes out of the house, only to come back with a desktop, monitor, console, everything.

"You going to bring in a printer too?" I ask him.

"Computer games," he tells me. "You play?"

"I hate video games with my whole heart." Having watched exceedingly fuckable dorks expend all their masculine energies into what their two thumbs could do in front of a screen instead of going outside or trying to pass their classes without academic probation or wooing likewise fuckable women like myself throughout high school, college, and a Ph.D. program, I decided early on that gaming was a dealbreaker, if for no other reason than this: I could not stomach the competition. More accurately, competing with a non-sentient device for a man's attention was bad for my self-esteem. When Luc made it clear that he preferred games of the mental-mind-fuck kind to anything that could be purchased in a 7x5" plastic case, saying yes to marriage became a no-brainer. Also, he was the only one who bothered to ask.

Then Sam started playing *Fortnite* three weeks into the latest pandemic, when purchasing an Xbox seemed preferable to murder-suicide, and within another fortnight (fifteen days exactly) I had lost my academicky, nice fourth grader to the great abyss where punks reside with their many virtual weapons and skins. Now that the virus has been relegated to the same status as the chicken pox—sporadic, rare, and usually not deadly—Luc and I take turns each week threatening to do unconscionable things to the Xbox while Sam is asleep whenever he misses too many math problems in a row or forgets to apply PEMDAS. The impending violence keeps my hatred of video games alive.

Duri knows none of this but is already convinced he can change a woman's mind. He has this look that I can only describe as amusement: a smile paired with eyes that do not believe a single word that has just been said.

"You like *Just Dance*," he hypothesizes.

"Are you asking me or predicting the future?"

He grabs the phone out of my hand and magically unlocks it himself when he correctly guesses what is apparently the most stupidly popular password the world over, "Zero, zero, zero . . . ?" His voice trails off as he thumbs the same digit over and over again. "Jja-jan!"* By the time he hands it back, there's a new app installed: a disco ball overlaid with the kind of block lettering typically reserved for YA novels and yard sales.

"What am I supposed to do with this?"

"Controller," he answers, pressing the power button on his monitor and console, which turn on with a speed I have never witnessed in any personal computing device. Maybe that's also what fame and fortune eliminate: the need to wait and waste time. A few clicks later, "Despacito" starts emanating from all three screens at once—the monitor, Duri's phone, mine—the harmonic progression of four highly recognizable chords activating some primitive muscle memory in the joint where hips meet pelvis, an urge as old as time (is that urge sex or music?).

"¿Conoces a Luis Fonsi?" I know nothing about the lives of global superstars, but I have an unfounded suspicion that they all know each other, the same way all Marvel and DC superheroes appear to

---

*Ta-da!

be always apprised of each other's comings and goings and are there-fore able to assemble at a moment's notice.

Duri squints. "Spanish?" Then, "I speak poquito." A pause. "No Luis. ¡Que lastima!"

Before I can ask him where he picked up Spanish—later, I'd hear about The Band's belated Latin America tour, waylaid originally by the pandemic—Duri starts gyrating while staring intensely at the Technicolor monitor, his phone in a death grip. He nods for me to do the same, and when I do, a second avatar emerges on the display, one whose outline is a demand to be copied, with spinning numbers that reflect how this game of monkey see, monkey do is going. Despite being an international sensation who can sing and dance on demand, perreo doesn't seem to be his thing. The PG-13 version on the screen borrows most of its moves from tango and salsa, replacing the exaggerated grinding/twerking that made the original music choreography so watchable with more generic hip undulations from side to side and flailing arms in every which direction.

I sway. I try to trace an invisible Hula-Hoop with my ass and draw numbers in the air with my shoulders, *A Beautiful Mind* but for the kinetically inclined. I try to forget the existence of children and husbands and my own age. When all else fails, I rely on old salsa moves and that one number from *Moulin Rouge* that I used to corrupt the nice Christian boys of Campus Crusade for Christ—back when "Crusade" was an acceptable name for a campus group and all dancing was considered a highly aggressive mating ritual that was tied to the devil by virtue of its imminent association with sex. They worked then, and surprisingly, they work now too: by the end of the song, my number is higher than Duri's. His screen pronounces me the winner.

He mumbles something into his phone, still in his hand, and the device translates back: "I am a man. As a woman, you are naturally better at these types of moves."

"You picked the song," I remind him.

He shrugs. In English, he says, "Song, good. But too sexy. I cannot do it."

This might be the biggest lie he's said all day. "They pay you millions of dollars to be sexy on a stage, and you always deliver. You sing, dance, and flirt with everything that moves. How many fans do you guys have again?"

Duri shakes his head before speaking into his phone once more. The ensuing translation: "I—we—have fans, yes. But do you know how many people called me on my birthday?"

"I did hear about that controversial song of yours—"

Duri tells his device, and his device tells me this: "It was before the song, which did not get posted until midnight. Right before I went to bed, I checked my phone. I got three messages wishing me a happy birthday. One from my mother, one from my brother, and one from my friend from high school who I have not seen since I debuted seven years ago."

"It's hard to be friends with a genius. They're usually too busy. I imagine it's also hard to be a genius with friends. Real ones, at least, who remember to ring you on your birthday."

"Genius is Gwangju. I'm the visual, remember?"

"Genius, talent, it's all the same thing. What I mean is, relationships require maintenance, loads of it. So much so that unless you share a gene pool or real estate or some other unavoidable reason to see each other and stick together, relationships are near impossible. Kids, apparently, are good at it for reasons I'm too old to remember. Elderly people are too, or so I hear, so that's something to look forward to, I guess? But everyone else in between doing the whole love-takes-work business is very, very tired.* Meanwhile, talent requires

---

*Tell me, then, is it any surprise that cheating has been around as long as love has? Because if relationships are work, then an affair is either a strike or a vacation depending on how it starts or—more importantly—how it ends.

the kind of total submission that tends to destroy everything else in its path. You're busy conquering the world. When do you have time to make friends?"

"You have job?" Duri asks in English.

"Psychologist," I tell him. "Not private practice," I clarify quickly, always afraid of the assumptions that follow—namely, that I can read minds or tell the future, two burdens I would wish on no one, least of all myself. "I teach college students. When I'm not doing that, I do research."

"Research?"

"On Asians and white people mostly." And the incomprehensible things they do—this I do not say.

Duri brightens. "You study me."

"You think you're that interesting?"

He smiles because he knows, apparently, that the answer is yes. With no accent whatsoever, he says with a kind of drawl, "You have no idea."

9

Therapy (D-5)

Duri's smile is short lived, though his prophecy rings true. I do end up studying the Pretty Boy, but not for the reasons either he or I hoped.

Twelve hours later, Duri is still sleeping, prostrated across the exceedingly hard guest bed with his door half open, privacy being a uniquely American value maybe. My parents also sleep with their bedroom double doors open, no matter who is in the house. I stand in the door jamb wondering when would be the appropriate time to take his pulse. Is the boy dead? Fifteen minutes later, when I check on him again, his position has shifted, a sign of life: he is now wrapped up in a burrito, tucked against the wall, only an onyx tuft of hair peeking out from the duvet covers.

The house is emptied of Luc and small children, who all have places to be for both their sakes and mine: a poorly rated charter school thirty miles away where Luc teaches physical education and where my children mostly educate themselves in front of screens well-stocked with videos that promise to instruct them on everything from algebra to climate change. The school is located in a town overridden with artificial turf and the nouveau riche—immigrants who have newly made it within the last decade and can therefore afford houses (cheap enough to buy in that neighborhood) but not the required landscaping to go with them.

At the fourteen-hour mark, because he hasn't moved, I hover a palm over Duri's lower face—the only part of his body exposed, the rest of him still in burrito. From the reflection in the wall-length mirrors doubling as closet doors, it looks like I am attempting a miracle that involves the laying on of hands in a post-#MeToo era where pastors are only allowed to pretend to touch congregants while desperately urging Father God to do his thing, pronto, please, thank you, Jesus. In this fantasy Hallmark Christmas movie, Duri is Lazarus, wrapped up in dressing, sashaying with death, about to be risen so he can die another day or hitch a ride to the thereafter some way that involves less heartbreak and fewer women crying. He seems to be breathing, I think? My palm detects air circulation, but I am no prophet.

Sixteen hours: Virtual office hours have come and gone, my only visitor the same Vietnamese kid who shows up every other week to talk about anything except the material I've recorded for class. This week he shows me, not in this order: the spring rolls he perfected last weekend for Lunar New Year; a video of his dance troupe's dragon performance, all giant animal eyes and fur and legs; his latest iPhone, refurbished, from Amazon; his hopes and dreams for the future, which have nothing to do with majoring in psychology but everything to do with being lead sales associate at Macy's, maybe even manager one day if he's lucky. Based on the intonation of his speech, I can tell it's not a crush driving this excess of self-disclosure and persistent interest in seeing my face on a screen. I doubt he likes my gender. Regardless of their other predilections, all boys appear to enjoy being mommied.

Sixteen and a half hours. Say what you want about crazy women, but you have to give us this: we get the job done. I remove all the metal pans from their storage spot in the oven, bumping into as many sur-

faces as possible along the way. Granite islands don't chip, what do
I care? Lift up, then put back down the cast-iron pan atop the grill,
adjust the overweight lid of the Le Creuset pot from yesterday, exposed lip rubbing against exposed lip. The fridge doors don't make
enough noise, and relying on the garbage disposal is too shameless—
even psychotics feel shame, the Asian ones, at least—so the Vitamix
comes out instead. There is no real blendable fruit in the house, just
two oranges macerating on the counter, their dimpled peels showing
their age, so I rinse both and plop them whole into the blender. This
indeed looks rather wrong, so to cover up the crime—does anyone
other than the nice folks at Orange Julius blend oranges?—I add some
spinach and kale to the mix. I remember seeing a demo at Costco
where the man behind the five-hundred-dollar blender did precisely
this—drop a conglomeration of unpeeled citrus (grapefruits, lemons,
limes) and bagged greens into the vortex before him and press "pulse,"
yielding a forest-colored concoction that both the pot-bellied cus-
tomers at Southern California's most popular warehouse and myself
found irresistible. Perhaps this is not as crazy as it sounds. I, too, press
"pulse" and use the phalange to stab the fruits into submission. Now
the kitchen smells like grass with a hint of citrus.

It works! Either the furious grinding of 2.2 peak horsepower
meets Vitamix's propriety in-built cooling fan or the fragrance of pul-
verized lawn did the trick. Duri, squinting at the witch's brew in my
hand, emerges in the kitchen like an apparition, pale and puffy and
as deadly as ever.

"Harry Potter?" he asks, narrowing the distance between us on
socked feet.

"Excuse me?" If I stay very still, maybe he'll keep moving and
eventually get close enough to touch, thanks to the enclosed space
that is my kitchen.

"Looks like 'Drink of Despair,'" he observes, still an arm's length
away. "So green."

"There's also coffee." I point to the contraption I bought Luc for our last anniversary, "a barista in a stainless-steel box," the blurb on the Williams-Sonoma Christmas catalog had said. It cost the equivalent of paying an actual Starbucks employee to work a forty-hour week for two months. You do the math; that's how much I love my husband. Or maybe that's how much I want my husband to think that he is loved. And/or that's how much I want to think I love my husband. *Cray-cray* doesn't even begin to capture the shadows in my head. As I tell Luc: "You couldn't survive for two hours inside me without losing your own goddamn mind."

He asks me: "Is that a good thing or bad thing?"

Then, his secondary observation: "That sounds like you have a magical vagina."

"I was talking about my head, silly, not my cunt," I always remind him.

"The two parts of you I love best," he replies. Maybe I do love my husband. At least, I love to be loved by him.

Duri, though, does not inquire after Luc or Sam or Kilim, only sits down on the counter stools on the other side of the kitchen island and glances at me patiently.

"You want breakfast," I guess.

A pretty hand flies to his mouth. He giggles, clutching his stomach. Is the man guffawing? "You want to be servant," he volleys.

Luc tells me all the time that I'm on the autism spectrum, so bad am I at reading between the lines. You tell me whether Duri is patronizing, joking, flirting, or demanding food. Then he confesses, "Not hungry. Never."

"You ate tteokbokki last night," I remind him.

"That was for you." This might be the nicest thing anyone has ever said to me, I decide.

"Thank you?" Then, "What exactly would you like?"

He looks around, but the effort of glancing at each individual object in the kitchen seems like too much work; he gives up by the time his saccades reach the sink and says, "I go back to sleep."

"Are you jet-lagged or something?"

"I always sleep twelve, thirteen hours. Fourteen. Sixteen sometimes."

"Since when?" The average person sleeps eight to nine hours a night: human beings may be wonderfully diverse when it comes to everything else—starting with how we like our eggs in the morning and ending with the precise level of kink we are willing to tolerate before bed—but when it comes to circadian rhythms, there is no room for creativity; we're all the same. Except, of course, when something goes wrong.

"Months. Year? On tour, no, of course, no time, but at home, no tour, yes. I sleep a lot."

"Did you stay up late playing *Just Dance* by yourself or something?" I mean it as a joke and reach across to smack him in the arm (or maybe, just maybe, to break the touch barrier), but Duri's face looks placid, as if stuck in a calm a person cannot easily recover from.

"Games not very fun anymore. I do not play very much."

"Other than sleeping, what do you like to do?"

"I like . . ." Duri pauses and glances around as if he has forgotten what it means to want. "I like . . ."

"Exercising? Playing guitar? Cooking things other than tteok-bokki?" I am racking my brain for things The Band have mentioned in their interviews, but it's beginning to dawn on me that watching famous people answer questions from a stranger may be the least illuminating thing they do and about as informative as combing a novel for autobiographical details from its author.

Duri scoffs. "Piano," he says. "I never play guitar."

"You love playing piano?" As one of those kids who started the keyboard at three in a Communist-era tenement in Nanking and stopped at sixteen after finally convincing my parents that practicing piano and maintaining a perfect GPA across five AP classes while also aiming for a perfect SAT score and being vice president of at least one after-school club were mutually exclusive, I did not know it was possible to love this instrument that every other Asian person I knew merely tolerated.

"No, I am no good at it."

"You are also no good at this game," I observe. "But it's more fun to be a little bad at something than too good at it. Then it's no fun at all."

"I am a little bad at everything and too good at nothing."

"Now that's just demonstrably false."

"Gwangju is the smart one. Genius, they call him. Min is the leader who speaks English like American after watching American TV. I watch same channel and still talk like this. Yoojin and Jae see dance one time, then can do it. Also, Yoojin can sing girl parts, his voice so good he might as well be angel. Jae has dimples."

"And you—"

"I'm Pretty Boy." Anti-fans have long whined about Duri's supremely flattering view of himself and shameless self-promotion with this self-titled moniker, but apparently they do not understand that the textbook definition of a narcissist is someone who wobbles constantly between extremely high and extremely low self-esteem.

"You're also—"

"The Eldest."

"Vocalist too!"

"Not primary."

"It's a competition?"

"No, but you wonder why no one is here knocking on door or calling phone, looking for me."

"Would you rather be doing something else with your life?"

"I would rather do nothing. Be done with everything."

"You mean—?"

"Don't worry," Duri says.

"Do you have a therapist you can tell these things to?" These days, you don't even have to be a licensed psychologist to be familiar with the signs; a cursory hobby for TED talks can be enough to familiarize a person with the common colds of the brain, when all that miraculous machinery stumbles across a single short circuit, or some particular gift passed down from ancestor to son encoded along a string of chromosomal letters —AA, bb—meets a series of unfortunate events, thereby fulfilling the ancient recipe for illness, diathesis meets stress. Spend enough time around people with classifiable mood disorders and you realize that what the suicidal person really wants is not to die per se—it takes effort to die these days, at least in the first world, where we generally lack lions and tigers and bears and random aerial drone attacks and cartel assassinations and civil wars—but rather, just to cease to be for however long or short of a period of time it takes for them to get some relief from the compulsively addictive thinking going on inside their own head.

Duri looks at me, and I know the answer is: it doesn't matter; yes or no doesn't change his current state or his future need. If he does go to therapy, it hasn't helped; if we could cure ourselves with our degrees and medications and faithful belief that truth is something always findable via randomized clinical trials or double-blind experiments, we'd all live forever. Nardil saved David Foster Wallace until it didn't, and he suspended himself from an exposed beam meant to hold up his house and not hang up his life, in a lovely tree-lined town named Claremont forty-seven miles from here, where Duri is sitting.

All of a sudden, it is hard not to clutch my own sternum in search of something to squeeze or anything to say to this boy, who, through the kind of hard work nerds and overachievers like myself can only dream of, managed to scale the tallest monuments known to men: worldwide fame, glory, worship by the young, admiration from the old, Grammys, Billboards, MNET, MAMA, iHeartRadio, IPOs, imitation in the absence of duplication, the pride of their countrymen, the respect of outsiders who heretofore had never given two thoughts to this little peninsula of a country dangling from China into the East Sea. His was a country that had invented neither gunpowder nor pasta nor philosophy nor Western civilization but instead, at the turn of the second millennium, managed to do something much more exciting: convince the world that Asians were now cool, and their men could be known for something other than dick size, and their talents extend beyond math and following directions. But having scaled the kind of heights reserved only for dreams, he can't help but look down from the apex, wondering what to do with himself next.

"You should see someone," I say. "A professional."

"I see you."

"I'm not a practicing psychologist, remember? Just a psychology professor!" But it's a familiar refrain, one I've heard before. In high school, I was so good at listening and rationing out sage advice for my girlfriends' idiotic infatuations that they all told me I should be a therapist when I grew up. *Then I'd have to charge you*, I'd remind them. *Anyhow, I don't like requiring people to pay for what friends should be doing for free.*

But once at Berkeley, it became apparent that I was not Asian enough for premed or male enough for engineering or gave enough shits for political science. For a single semester sophomore year, I briefly tried out Political Economics of Industrialized Societies, but the 800-page-a-week readings for its introductory class led by an itsy blonde woman who talked tirelessly for seventy-five minutes without a single visual or PowerPoint slide was sufficient to kill off that idea. History was too close to home after a prolonged emotional affair with my high school history teacher, whose love letters on the margins of my AP essays I carried around like a phantom limb long into adulthood, one that would never amount to anything physical until jail time was out of the question but still managed to cause so much longing that here I am now, bringing him up again. English Lit I liked, but it was too easy, the temptation to bullshit too appealing, so I chose Spanish Lit instead. Because even Borges and Juan Rulfo could not elucidate the incomprehensible things I felt, thought, and wanted, I took a psychology class by a middle-aged Chinese professor with a Beijing accent so thick and layered that we all couldn't help but hang on every word he said in the hopes of understanding every other. One class turned into two. By the time my cap and gown arrived, it listed two majors in my commencement catalog: Psychology and Spanish Literature. I had no interest in working a nine-to-five job like the peons around me, so I kept going: graduate school, post-docs, tenure track. I stayed away from private practice because an elderly white gentleman taught us in Psych 1 that therapy doesn't always work. As far as I could tell, this was the equivalent of finding out that Santa wasn't real or that the Bible might have a typo. Blame the naïveté that's pretty much a prerequisite for being in your early twenties. I had no interest in a future working with people I could not save.

"You have the money to pay for it," I tell Duri. This is an asinine observation, of course. "I'm not Korean, but I know how to google. We could find someone local for you to talk to."

A noise escapes his nose, the universal sound of calling someone a twit, maybe? "I have the money," he confirms, repeating my words. "That, the problem."

"What? Money can't be the cause of your problems." The issue with being a smart person with a Ph.D. is that you start to believe everything you read in books, provided that it has an adequate citation from a peer-reviewed source and is written by people from degree-granting institutions. Science is iterative, but no one recalls the *oops*. Remember phrenology, fen-phen, the blank slate, behaviorism? Of course not, at least not with any clarity or remorse. Even Einstein famously referred to quantum entanglement as that "spooky" thing in the distance. Maybe I should've listened to Notorious B.I.G. instead.*

---

*Mo' money, mo' problems, no?

Case in point: money makes people happy (studies show). Life is no Hallmark card; there's nothing like cold hard green to make a divorce palatable or make your children love you for a season or a day or convince someone outside your league that what you lack in good looks you make up for in expensive gadgets and toys. Maybe these studies neglected to include international megastars whose face can sell out any product in the known universe, be it vitamins or bedroom furniture, who've spent the last seven years maintaining music's longest winning streak via a nonstop tour schedule involving two album releases a year and three separate reality television series plus an endless stream of free content for YouTubers who will watch a whole hour of this boy and his comrades do the most boring of tasks: sit in airport lobbies, blow up balloons, deliver monologues from hotel rooms, wait for dinner to be delivered. I should know; I've done it too, a habit I find only slightly more embarrassing than scrolling through *Bridgerton* just for the porno scenes.

Duri doesn't bother to answer. He gets out his phone and taps the blue bird with the green beak. "You have not seen what I have seen," the app translates.

"You've witnessed some horrible things?" This I haven't heard before. According to all the online profiles, each member's life started during the handful of pubescent years leading up to their debut, before which nothing of significance ever happened, just a long stretch of waiting and wanting. Since then, it's been an even longer parade of rainbows and butterflies, interrupted only occasionally by some sasaeng or fringe group of anti-fans or a wayward reporter's accusations costumed as pointed questions; blips, really, on the staircase to heaven.

"The opposite. Last year I saw the beaches of Redondo Beach—that is close to here, no?"

"Fifteen minutes—"

"—get outdone by the beaches of Rio and Barcelona. Right before we debuted The Band, we took a trip to Los Angeles, this was before there were H Marts everywhere, and when I sat in the sand at Redondo Beach, I told Gwangju, this must be heaven—"

"I always thought Redondo Beach's water looked a little like bathwater," I told him. In the competition for biggest snob, there are always multiple winners.

"You are right, it is not heaven, because now I have seen the glacier-formed lakes in New Zealand, so blue Gwangju asked me if maybe the sea here should be jealous. I have been in a lot of stadiums, really big ones, where the people look like stars in the sky, they are so far away. I have met Taylor Swift and know how tall she is, so tall in person! I have met Shawn Mendes and know how handsome he is, even more handsome than on a screen. I have been asked by every American interviewer which American musician I want to collaborate with. I know the cell phone number of Drake. I have had two million people post birthday wishes for me online, and I did not recognize a single one of them by name. I have seen female idols up close, and I know this now: There are women in this world who are beautiful in a way that is not human, beautiful in a way that makes me hold my breath because I am terrified. They do not look like anyone I have ever met growing up in Daegu. I cannot imagine them drinking soup or having a bowel movement because it feels so impossible. I cannot even fantasize about them—"

"You sound very deep, because I have no problem fantasizing about overly attractive people," I tell him. This is very, very true. At the risk of sounding like I'm appropriating what men of all sexual orientations have been doing since Adam first discovered he could skull-fuck Eve, I have to admit there is something erotic about a man on the verge of falling apart, at least if this man has shoulders you could hang yourself on and above-average height and lips that resemble fruit (cherries, loquats, mangosteen) in addition to status, money, bilateral symmetry. Or God forbid, the voice of an angel, which apparently can cover a multitude of sins. If anything, falling apart may be a secret source of sex appeal for men,* who as a species appear to fall apart so rarely in front of an audience that when they do, it's like some rare astronomical event that happens once every couple of decades. Witnessing it feels like being chosen. Besides, as women have been told for as long as men have been around, there are no difficult men anyway, just men who need to be taken care of. Like the one on my counter stools.

Duri isn't done. "I have spent five hundred American dollars on a ring from a souvenir stand that I wore for two hours. I have thrown away three cell phones over the course of one summer because I did not like their buttons. I have lost more AirPods than the fingers on my hands and so have stopped counting."

"Cam Newton—do you know who he is? NFL quarterback? American football? He said once that he's spent a million dollars on clothes he's worn only once. And JC Chasez—from NSYNC? The boy band that wasn't the Backstreet Boys? He told Rosie O'Donnell—she's a talk show host, was one, I mean—that he wears underwear once and then throws it out, because he finds used underwear disgusting." I don't know why I'm telling Duri this.

"What happened to this Cam and JC?"

"Early retirement."

"Do you mean—? Is that a euphemism?" Duri makes a motion circling his own neck, then tugs at an invisible rope in the air.

"Oh God, no, that's not what I mean at all! They're both alive and well. Last I checked. Alive, at least, that I'm almost positive. When a famous person dies, there is always a news story."

"Are they happy now?" Duri appears to be serious. Either he thinks I'm Madame Cleo by virtue of my psychological training or—more likely—he thinks I actually know these two guys because of the intimate details I've revealed about their credit card bills and undergarment drawers.

---

*Psychologists have even come up with a term for this; see: the Pratfall Effect.

"That I don't know."

Duri's face falls a little. The little pockets under his eyes deepen and cast crescent-shaped shadows on his cheeks.

"Are you saying you miss those things? You want to go back and be on tour again?" I ask him.

"Do you know what the best thing about being on tour is?"

"The groupies?" I've always wondered if K-pop idols took advantage of their unparalleled access to people who want to have sex with them the same way other musicians have (ever since David played his harp and it pleased the Lord so much he got made king, with all its carnal perks).

"Americans may do it for the women, but no, for me it is the parenting."

"You already have parents. I have never heard an Asian person say they wish their parents parented them more."

"You do not understand. Every choice and action is decided for us ahead of time by people who know what they are doing and get paid to do it nicely. I never have to make a choice and never have to wonder if I will live to regret my decision, because I did not make it. Staff members wake us up in the mornings. They pick food out of our teeth before we show up anywhere where there might be a camera. The stylists dress us most of the time, food gets ordered ahead of time, it is all free, of course, but we know better than to eat too much. Jae gets away with it because he is the youngest and the most talented and naturally has a six-pack given to him by God, but everyone else notices when your face gets puffy the next morning from the sodium—"

"This is a problem, is what you're saying?"

"It is not a problem until the tour ends. Then everything requires a level of intent, of planning—agency, is it?—that I do not know how to muster anymore. There are no people to make certain that I do things or show up places or eat or sleep—"

"That's supposed to be relaxing. You know that, right? Getting to do nothing."

"There is nothing relaxing about despair."

"You are depressed."

"I am—I am—I—" Duri looks around my kitchen as if I am the one hiding the secret answers to life. "I am dissatisfied. I cannot help it. I do not care how much I like to cook. It is never going to taste like anything made by a chef with a star next to his restaurant in the tour books. When I air-dry my own hair, I can barely look at myself in the mirror. I do not know how to make those little corners on the edges of the bed the way hotels do it. Taylor Swift is taller than me in heels, and Shawn Mendes looks the same without makeup. I am not going to call Drake because really, what would I say? My English is not good enough—"

"You sound—"

"Do I look depressed to you?" On cue, Duri contorts his face into a grin, all teeth and cheekbone. I don't know what my own face is doing, but whatever it is, he appears to find it immensely amusing: he spanks his own knee with one hand while pointing at me with the other, letting out a condensed noise resembling a chuckle.

"Is that a trick?" I ask him.

"I am laughing."

"Yes, but are you depressed?"

"I can laugh and be depressed at the same time?"

"As I tell undergrads, Asians can apparently look at depression and laugh in its face."

"Eh?"

"They did a whole study on it. Got a bunch of depressed Asians and white people to watch a funny movie clip. And they videotaped the responses to see how everyone reacted."*

---

*See: Chentsova-Dutton et al. 2010.

Duri only squints, so I pull up my favorite emotion elicitation clip* on YouTube and turn on the auto-captioning.

"I apologize ahead of time if it makes you uncomfortable," I tell him.

"This is movie?"

"Of course. Even in America, what this woman is about to do next would never happen in real life."

Duri watches the screen, and I watch him, his pupils darting between young Billy Crystal and younger Meg Ryan. When a third guttural breath escapes her mouth—*ooohh AAAhhh*—Duri looks up at me with an expression I can't place. Wonder, maybe, or disbelief? Either that or he is too offended to speak. By the time she is full on banging the restaurant table, crying *yes yes YES* into her sandwich, simulating the world's most convincing fake orgasm just to prove a point, Duri is straight up shaking, an arm wrapped around his diaphragm and a giant hand covering his face, which is scrunched up like a child's; he's never looked more Asian. God, I hope he is laughing and not crying. God answers my prayer because just then, he emits a bleat. The full force of the noise interrupts the silent short breaths he's been taking, an act of violence not unlike an orgasm, come to think of it—the real kind and not the fake one that Meg Ryan has simulated so convincingly onscreen. He's laughing.

"You've never seen this movie, I take it?"

Duri swipes his eyes, which don't look particularly wet to me. Is he fake crying? "Let's watch whole thing," he says in English. "Funny funny."

"Okay. But I've got to tell you: you did exactly what the depressed Asians in the study did."

"What I do?"

---

*The infamous orgasm diner scene from *When Harry Met Sally* is among the top two films for eliciting amusement (Gross and Levenson 1995), albeit the original study mentioned here relied on a different one—an unnamed clip about a comedian going to the dentist.

"You laughed harder. Depressed white people were not terribly amused, much less amused than their non-depressed counterparts who watched the same funny video clip. But Asians laughed more when they were depressed. Non-depressed Asians smiled but kept their calm, probably in line with cultural norms about modesty and group harmony and not drawing too much attention to yourself. But those who were despairing—it's funny, their despair made them go against what all the other Asians in the room were doing, made them break all the social rules they normally live by. Maybe because that's what depression tells you: that there's nothing left to lose and there-fore nothing left to follow."*

Duri brings his phone up to his lips and whispers this: "Every in-terview they ask the same questions. The fans too—I love them, but they all want to know the same things. Am I okay, who am I dating, and if I am not dating anyone, what kind of girl do I like, what am I going to do next, why did I say this, why did I do that? At a certain point, if I revisit my feelings or thoughts anymore, they are going to die on me, they are going to wither from excessive use, from being talked about to the point of exhaustion. A joke is not funny the second time you tell it, but my opinions and preferences and memories—it is like that too, they also get warped the more I talk about them, they lose their original shape and meaning. So please don—"

"Oh, honey," I say, reaching for him because secretly and deep down, I've always wanted to be one of those handsy white women who can hug anyone and never get called inappropriate (or worse). "We don't have to talk. We can do something else."

---

*They call this the "cultural norm hypothesis" (see: Chentsova-Dutton et al. 2007).

10

We All Saw It Coming

On the other side of the Pacific, Pinocchio—remember him?—wakes up the following morning and discovers this note underneath his office door:

I'M COMING FOR YOUR SECOND BABY. Standard A4 computer paper, 8.25x11.7, 12-point font, typed out, unsigned.

He laughs. Is this a joke? He hasn't screwed anything but his own hand in years—the model girlfriend is on the horizon but not there yet—and the two or three times he's managed to get a woman to sit on him previously, he was always careful, so careful: condom, spermicide, the works. Perhaps "baby" is not meant to be taken literally here. Perhaps, like other men known for their workaholism or preternatural talents, their babies have virtually nothing to do with their biological seed—who at best only share 50% of their DNA and have annoying minds and needs of their own—and everything to do with the work of their hands, which is entirely their own creation and therefore subject to their total creative control.

"You know anything about this?" he asks his secretary, a former comedian turned case study on the side effects of plastic surgery done too well (in her case, a physical package so breathtaking no one could laugh at her jokes anymore, not because the surgeries made her any less funny but because audiences are supremely bad at multitasking and could not process punch lines while checking out the woman they were coming from at the same time). So she transitioned to the kind of job historically reserved for beautiful women: administrative assistant.

"What's that?" she asks, blinking profusely, another side effect of having three surgeries on two eyes. "Your mail?"

"Never mind." Pinocchio closes his door and asks himself why he should bother with a pretty secretary if his own company policy prohibits workplace romance—originally set in place to prevent overzealous sasaengs from applying for a staff job for the sole purpose of infiltrating the machinelike bubble that is The Band—but surely a rule that applies to him as well. He tosses the paper and does not think about it until much later, when it comes back to explain a few things.

He summons the remaining four members of The Band to his office.

Min is the first to show up because he is the type of person whose responsibility makes up for his lack of warmth. Gwangju and Yoojin are close behind. Jae, last.

"Your hair," Pinocchio says.

All the members look at Jae, who for the first time since they've known him is sporting a different hair color than what his mother bequeathed him. Flaxen—though normally reserved to describe the sexually charged tresses of pubescent blonde girls of Scandinavian or Germanic origin—also fits him now. The dye job is recent enough that even the roots of his hair are the color of corn muffins.

"You like it," Jae replies. It is not a question, merely a statement, because having acquired a furious following of international female fans (and an equally furious share of international male fans) since he was thirteen, he expects unwavering adoration. He can't even post a selfie in bad bedroom lighting without breaking the internet, so this is less about cockery and more about an empirical extrapolation from past facts.

"Next time, ask me," Pinocchio suggests.

Asians trained in the fine art of indirect communication will know that all suggestions of future behaviors are indictments of past sins. Still, Jae is young—only twenty-three; Jae is a puppy. He understands nothing and therefore always manages to emerge blameless. "You know how to dye hair?"

The boss man waves the air, tired already. "Duri," he says instead.

"We haven't heard from him." Even when he doesn't need to, Min likes to speak for the group.

"The real question is: What would we do if we had?" Pinocchio corrects.

"You mean, besides ask him where he is?"

"And when he's coming back?" Yoojin adds.

"If we want him to come back." Another correction, by the only man in the room authorized to do so.

Yoojin stands up just as Gwangju snatches his sleeve, but all that happens is an exposed collarbone, the happy byproduct of a stretch tee's forgiving collar. "This is what we've come here to debate?"

"He is thirty." Age is often the answer, even if the question itself varies.

"You are how old?" Yoojin asks.

"I get to be both old and ugly and it does not matter one iota. No one recognizes my face and pays extra for juice boxes because I am on them. You and I, we have different problems," Pinocchio replies.

"I thought locating Duri was our shared problem."

"He is your friend, you miss him. I understand human affection." On this, Pinocchio is probably fibbing; anyone who has to use the term "human" in front of a word like "affection" is likely neither all that human nor that affectionate. "But at this point The Band is less a group of boys and more a nation-state with a lot of vested interests at stake."

"The IPO," Gwangju reminds him. "We each have our shares."

"Correction: I own 33.4 percent, and all five of you together do not come close."

"But the board—"

"You have been watching too many American television shows. The board is happiest when they know nothing."

"Do you know something we don't?" Min inquires.

"I am trying to."

"A private investigator?" Jae, who has seen more television of both American and Korean varieties than bookish Gwangju, appears interested by this prospect.

"Do not worry your pretty little head. You are not paying for it."

"Ah, see, I knew you liked my new hair."

"Can't we just track his credit card bills? Tap his phone or something? Trace his calls, at least? It's a minimum." Jae is showing us all that he has learned.

"We're idols, dummy, not the National Intelligence Service or the FBI," Gwangju interjects but then looks to Pinocchio for confirmation. "Right?"

"Duri left the phone Samsung gifted you all behind. The number has been dead for a while. I think the man's gone through three phones in three months. The last one he must have bought himself. It is not on any company expense sheets. And Hyundai, say what you want about their cars, but when it comes to the Black Card, they are pretty discreet; they tell you nothing about their clientele and what they are using it on."

"We're fucked." Jae never asks questions, only throws statements against walls to see if they stick.

"Are we?" Gwangju asks.

The three remaining members swivel their heads in his direction.

"What?" he says. When he blinks multiple times in a row—a facial tic—his right eyelid develops a crease, creating an asymmetry that under normal conditions is a sign of prenatal pathogen exposure, but in his case just makes him appear mysterious and therefore powerful, a useful defense akin to a camel's crazy curves or a pufferfish's trademark bloat. "The voice tracks we've been recording, all those photos we took for the label from every possible angle, full-body shots, close-ups. You're doing something with them, aren't you?"

When Pinocchio doesn't answer, Gwangju says, "You know, I saw a news story the other day. I didn't think anything of it until now. It said you bought an AI company. Artificial Intelligence. A Silicon Valley startup, some five thousand miles away."

The other members look to their impresario, who asks, "Do you know what Andy Warhol said his mission was?"

Min shakes his head, but Gwangju refuses to break Pinocchio's gaze, while neither Yoojin nor Jae appear to know who Warhol is.

"He wanted to paint like a machine," Pinocchio tells them. "It was less about art and more about production. His assistants helped. He even started signing the pictures they made before eventually just asking them to stamp his signature."

"Are you saying what I think you're saying?" Gwangju asks.

"Duri knows exactly where we are. If he is not here, he probably does not want to be. He is not hiding against his will."

"What if there's foul play?" Jae looks excited again: his eyes, already round, become rounder still, crowding out the rest of his face.

Pinocchio shakes his head. "If there was anything amiss, we would be having a different conversation. Then the National Intelligence Service would be involved, but there is nothing to suggest that."

"Maybe we should respect the man's wishes to be left alone?" Gwangju blinks some more, threatening to create a matching crease in his left eye.

Yoojin drops back into his chair. Min says nothing, only considers his footwear for signs of scuff. There are no right answers here, but potentially many wrong ones, so perhaps it is best for him to keep quiet and carry on. Pinocchio, however, never runs out of words.

"The schedule stays the same. We cancel nothing, and when interviewers ask, you can tell them the truth. We respect Duri's rest and recovery period—"

"What exactly do we say he's recovering from?" Yoojin inquires.

"I never told you what to say in interviews and I am not about to start now."

"Correction: We can't talk about girls. Past ones, maybe from high school and future ones in the generic, but no present and no recent past, nothing since debut." Jae, for which this rule requires the most self-restraint, says this matter-of-factly, but there is an edge to his voice, like someone's who just given a keynote speech but then is asked an obvious comment disguised as a question.

"That is less of a commandment and more of a fact of life, is it not? Name a Korean artist who willingly volunteers that information if not for some revelatory photo from Dispatch. You boys do not have time to date anyway." Pinocchio, like Jae, sometimes makes statements when he should be asking questions. Min's eyebrows ascend imperceptibly into his forehead, creating a soft wrinkle where there should be none. Gwangju's lips curl into one cheek, causing the beginning of a dimple, even in the absence of a smile. They say nothing.

"Dispatch and us, we have an agreement. A symbiotic relationship, as they say. We give them unlimited access to all the photo shoots they want, and they leave you alone when you have got your finger up your nose, or worse. You think it is magic that there's not a single photo of you with some girl on your arm floating around the world wide web? That level of oblivion you have to buy."

"I thought it's because we're always so careful." Even Min is surprised by this revelation that things are simply not what they seem.

"The Queen of England was careful, more careful than you, but look where it got her, even up to her passing: a stray grandson on the other side of the pond, living in their colony that got away, all because they could not work it out with the tabloids, first with his late mother, then his wife—"

"Who's more famous, though, us or them?" Jae wants to know.

"The Band does have more Twitter followers than the Royal Family. Instagram too."

The members nod, a moment of celebration that five small-town boys from Korean suburbs no non-Korean has ever heard of have managed to accrue more international fame and glory than an institution as old and revered as the British monarchy, but Pinocchio interrupts: "Aigoo—do you know anything about this?"

He fishes the typed paper out of the trash bin, passes it around. It still says I'M COMING FOR YOUR SECOND BABY, but it dawns on him now that it's written in English.

"You have kids?" Finally, a question out of Jae's mouth, but one he doesn't wait for an answer to. "I can't believe you've never mentioned him. Or is it a girl? It's too late for this, but congratulations." A beat. "Wait, you have a wife?"

"You are my kids."

Jae covers his mouth, capturing the laughter, but Gwangju observes, "By that logic, they're coming for us."

"Who's they?" Min says.

"Forget it." Pinocchio snatches the note back, drops it a second time in the bin. "You have security. Nothing has changed."

What do you call a statement that is both true and not true at the same time?

11

The Free World (D-4)

The next morning, the quartet of remaining Band members boards a commercial aircraft for a series of stops in miguk. Andrew used to say that Koreans invented everything, including the Chinese, but on this particular linguistic oddity, he was wrong: *miguk* came borrowed from *meiguo*, "beautiful country" in Mandarin, which refers to—what else—America.

It's their usual circuit, one they've done before: a daytime talk show, a surprise musical appearance on a comedy sketch program, then an awards show. It's the rock star's version of a long weekend spent in a duo of cities (Manhattan and Hollywood) whose matching insomnias are the best antidote for jetlag.

When the four boys arrive, entourage and all, at JFK, during one of those undecided hours between midnight and morning, there are only clumps of drowsy travelers—either workaholics on business, stuck with ill-timed but heavily discounted itineraries booked by vindictive or stupid secretaries, or else exceedingly cheap sojourners, happy to trade time and sanity for the most cost-effective red-eye flights. In either case, these are two groups unlikely to have the time or money to have seen The Band in concert and therefore disinclined to recognize them in public spaces when they are devoid of makeup and costumes and backup dancers.

The illusion that they can walk through a public airport unbothered evaporates the second the mob gathered at the bottom of baggage claim sees their feet peek out from the descending escalators, four separate pairs of leather and suede vegetable-tanned to colors of fruit: red, green, pink, blue. No one else wears shoes that nice to deboard a plane at five a.m., at least, no one else who shows up flanked in every direction by a racially homogenous group of men and women wearing every possible shade of black, interrupted occasionally only by a larger person in a yellow EVENT STAFF shirt.

The screaming begins, the hollering, crying, face-grabbing. Each boy's name gets screamed, repeatedly, with the kind of enthusiasm normally saved for orgasm. There is no question that teenage girls and their gay guy friends are single-handedly the best species at worship of the self-eviscerating kind. They are so good at it that it's a wonder there aren't entire cults made up of solely high school sophomores or theater kids. There's the occasional smattering of straight boys and even multiple fistfuls of moms eager to yell at men other than the ones they call husband. There are very few dads, who might go to a stadium at a reasonable evening hour to watch one of their protracted and exquisitely priced performances but will not, for the love of God, wake up in the middle of the night to catch a free glimpse of a stranger at the airport. Regardless, the collective adoration is loud enough to sound like fear—or Armageddon.

This part is old news for these boys who have yet to meet old age. They blink beneath their newsboy caps and umbrella hats and oversized hoodies and leave without so much as a goddamn carry-on, just the random man-bag, so light is the load they must be bearing. They have perfected the Princess Di wave: head ducked, as if shy, fingers touching, palm open, an invitation if there ever is one.

England may have twelve hundred years of monarchic rule, but the rest of the free world has The Band, who gives more content gratis than any working royal and demands less sympathy for their entrapment. Four matching Escalades idle outside along painted red curbs while two human centipedes of airport security form a tunnel leading straight from escalator to car doors, challenging the congregating fandom to a game of Red Rover, Red Rover, who dare send a girl on over?

In the Escalade, Jae asks, "Tell me what you're going to say."

Min is too smart to play dumb; he knows exactly what he's talking about. "You tell me; I'll say it."

Gwangju offers, "We say the exact same thing as when they ask us about girls."

"We give a different answer every time. Last time it was 'Do you know of any nice ones you'd like to introduce us to?' The audience went crazy for that. Before that, it was the standard 'We don't have time to date.' Or 'We feel so loved by our fans, we don't even feel the need to pursue love elsewhere for the time being,'" Min reminds him.

"Exactly. They all translate to the same thing: it's none of your goddamn business, so please stop asking, but if you must, I will deflect all you want."

"Are you suggesting I ask the host if he knows where Duri is?" Min inquires. "I don't think that joke will land."

"Americans take missing people very seriously," Gwangju agrees. "They put their faces on their milk bottles, I heard, and everyone looks very hard for them."

Min, who had studied Americans with an anthropological intensity since middle school, when his own exoskeleton felt like a foreigner and foreign land felt like a nice place to look for home, demanded, "Where did you hear this? I've never heard this."

"You know Usher? He has a whole song about it. 'Milk Carton,' it's called. *I'm about to put your face up on a milk carton,*" the Genius raps.

"How about: 'Duri is taking a break'?" Yoojin offers.

"'Break' implies he's coming back."

"You know something we don't?" Yoojin looks at Gwangju sharply. When they were trainees and starving for both aesthetic and socio-economic reasons, Duri would boil chicken breasts—bought on his own dime—and cut them into mouth-sized pieces, then sneak them into Yoojin's hand at random intervals during the day: between dance practices, amid bathroom breaks, occasionally before bed. The meat, tender and strange and wet, had to be eaten at once or else, and when Yoojin did with great bewilderment and gratitude, Duri would laugh like some kind of demented mama bird or fairy godmother who managed to summon all kinds of strange impossible things into being. The elder never did explain how he knew about the younger one's capacity to go for days without eating. Only now, in his absence, does Yoojin realize he hasn't eaten solid food in a week and a half.

"We know nothing, so let's not make promises we can't keep." Min, you can tell, will take over Pinocchio's job in a decade's time, so palpable is his ability to commandeer chaos and distill it into a single grain of brutal truth. Either that or Duri's disappearance feels like the existential equivalent of finding out his baby isn't his, a crisis that not only upends all present and future plans but also demands a rewriting of history and his own role in it—specifically, whether he, as the lead, should've foreseen it.

"Why don't you just say that? Look into the camera. Say those words exactly: *We know nothing.* Then add: *But we know this: We love you, Duri, we support you no matter what.*" Because Jae is still a child, he can afford to love the grown-ups in the room recklessly, with the kind of abandon age and its many sidekicks (wisdom, experience) will eventually breed out of him.

"You're going to sound like one of those parents whose child just disappeared, trying to speak to the local news channel." Gwangju sounds a little jealous. Considering that it took seven years of straight Billboard hits and winning a Grammy for his own father to show up at a concert, only to disappear at intermission, watching loving parents miss their children publicly and without shame or irony has always felt like pornography. For this reason, he understood Duri's controversial music video about faraway fathers unwittingly eating their desperate sons better than anyone else. Even now, watching the aftermath, a little part of Gwangju wishes it was him who wrote that song, if for no other reason than to go home after the long fall from grace and be able to say to his progenitor, "All this was for you."

"Technically, Duri has disappeared, and we are trying to communicate with him. Let's call it what it is."

"You think he'll be watching?" Jae asks.

"He better," Min mutters. "If I can't even break up with my exes without stalking them online for the better part of a year, Duri should not be able to get over us this quickly. He's only been gone for what, a week?"

"Ten days," Yoojin corrects, surprising everyone with this precision.

"By Sunday it'll be two weeks," Jae observes. "The anniversary of his disappearance. Anti-anniversary?"

"Maybe he'll surprise us," Yoojin offers, a little wistful. "Maybe he'll show up in time for the awards show, join us on stage like nothing happened."

"That would be a surprise all right," Min answers. Little do they know.

12

What Lennon Taught Us (D-3)

et's not forget the conditions under which Yoko Ono lost a husband and the rest of world lost the possibility of a Beatles reunion. John Lennon stepped out of a limo on W 72nd Street on New York's Upper West Side in a previously ordinary December during a *Monday Night Football* game. A fat kid in glasses reading a J. D. Salinger book earmarked the page where the word "phony" first appears before putting it down and replacing it with something arguably more compelling than a YA novel about some unhappy white boy waxing poetic about his hard-knock ennui: a .38 caliber revolver loaded with a sleeve of banned hollow-point bullets designed to shred a body before taking its life.

Five clicks later, Lennon is no longer breathing. Mark David Chapman becomes a name you and I now must know. His reasons for doing the incomprehensible are too asinine to commemorate here—"Glory," he said, forty years later, at his denied parole hearing. One person's shitty, miserable life could interrupt another person's full one at the precise moment when everyone's just watching the telly and no one is expecting assassination. You can't say I didn't warn you. Now, if you're surprised, it's not because you didn't see it coming.

The Escalades deposit the four Band members straight into the studio parking lot of the afternoon talk show with a rarity in American television: a popular and well-regarded female comedian whose warmth is not yet poised to be a threat to her competence. It's only seven a.m., but these guys do not fool around; like good Asian kids, they believe in practice more than they believe in fate. It doesn't matter that Jae can hit Bb5 notes during REM sleep or Yoojin uses body rolls—five in a row—to time how long to brush his teeth. Seven years in, they still rehearse every song, complete with choreography, before each performance. They remind their own bodies how to defy nature and do the impossible: sing, dance, and pout intensely into the camera at the same time without so much as letting the audience hear them breathing, not a single suck of air or breathy exhale even as the music winds down and the choreo deposits them in an abstract modernist heap in the center of the stage.

The congregation in the back lot is triple the size of the welcoming committee at the airport, but who's counting? When it comes to people, the human brain is not adequately designed to deeply process or care about quantities past the number of fingers we can count them with.* The stray sleeping bags strewn about might've given the crowd a transient quality were it not for all the lip gloss and highlighter and eye shadow. The amount of reflective material deposited on cheeks and brows and collarbones is sufficient to make them collectively shimmer like a well-populated school of rainbow fish. At least one white girl in the crowd whispers aloud,

---

*See: Collapse of Compassion studies (e.g., Slovic 2013).

"Wow, they look more Asian in person," and as she does, all the eyes around her turn into slits.

In the greenroom, Shake Shack burgers and milk shakes await, but no fries, since they age more badly than both ground sirloin and ice cream. Jae grabs one each and inserts half of the sandwich into his mouth before taking a long sip. Yoojin points at the white cream tinged with meat juice dribbling down the youngest member's chin and notes, "You look like a dirty old man who has just made a woman very happy."

"Ya," Gwangju says, because he understands the reference. "They're filming. This is going on YouTube later. Did you really just say that out loud?"

Yoojin glances around. He thinks about pussy to distract himself from thinking about meat. And ice cream. "No one speaks Korean except the people we brought ourselves."

"Everything is translated and captioned these days, you punk," Min replies. "My guess is we probably have more international fans at this point than Korean ones, even. Population-wise, there's no way it's even close."

Gwangju, who is naturally skinny and therefore insufferable, asks: "Did somebody eat all the fries already?"

Jae, who is apparently still hungry, replies: "Americans—or is it Canadians? The French? French Canadians? Who are the ones who dip French fries in ice cream?"

"Considering there are no fries here, no one does." Gwangju, irritated, goes back to his Nintendo Switch, the console the color of bridesmaid dresses (sea green, coral), the allure of helping avataristic animals cross off their checklist of daily activities on a virtual island irresistible, or at least preferable to eating cold American beef IRL.

Jae, now adequately fed, sits himself on an unclaimed chair and flutters his eyes closed. On cue, one of the funereally dressed women from the airport rushes over behind him, retrieving magically from her robe of many pockets a long wooden stick studded repeatedly with pointy knobs, its two ends sharpened to points. It looks like a weapon, or the kinkiest sex toy imaginable. She holds the ends in her fists and brings the club down toward his neck like a guillotine, but no one in the room appears to notice. Yoojin has joined Gwangju on the Switch, while Min appears to be in the middle of a dental exam, his mouth open and exposed to the recessed lights overhead while a man, also in black, stabs his incisors with a pair of toothpicks. At the same time, he is furiously typing on his phone, thumbs silently tap-dancing across the glass. Not even Jae himself is paying attention to his own spinal cord, that precious spot where cerebellum meets neck, where every boring repetitive movement crucial to the survival of the person housing them (breathing, heartbeat, temperature, balance) is controlled by a billion invisible puppet strings speaking to each other in electric whispers.

A guttural sound escapes from Jae's still-small mouth as the trio of sharp wooden objects sprouting from the stick take turns grinding into the symmetrical slopes of nape conjoined with shoulder. It remains unclear whether he is in pleasure or in pain, but regardless, he is surprised by none of it. The body may be a temple, but some bodies are more temples than others, and Jae's body—twenty-three and beautiful and so very good at following directions and making women cry—is used to being touched and prodded by unfamiliar people and objects meant to make him last a little longer.

"Aack," he says, a sound that needs no translation.

"You're making us blush," Yoojin calls out. "Stop it."

Jae's eyes are still closed. His mouth slinks across his chin, drooping a little. He is either asleep or dead, stuck in rigor mortis.

A producer pops in—everyone can tell because of the elaborate headpiece he has atop his coiffed head, paired with the shamelessly wrinkled combination of old denim meets new cotton, the universal getup for television station personnel with power but no free time. A duo of tweens and their middle-aged mothers trail after him.

"We've got a surprise!" he cries. It's unclear whether this announcement is directed toward The Band, who were not expecting any meet-and-greets, or the lucky quartet of ladies suddenly in their midst, who surely are. He pushes the women forward with the very tips of his fingers, trying to touch as little of their backs as humanly possible. Given all the recent allegations against his show in particular, and men in positions of power in general, a guy can never be too careful.

Min, the de facto leader in all situations requiring an English speaker, places his phone beneath his chair and looks up, forcing his previously placid face into a well-practiced grin, all dimples and eyebrow.

"Welcome, fans," he says in his characteristic baritone. Even though he is sitting, he still bows a little toward the moms, who giggle and for a brief and wondrous moment forget their age and their ex-husbands and their former racism and instead cannot help but think how young this guy looks, how perfect his eye makeup and how pillowy his lips, how charming an Asian accent is suddenly when you want to fuck the person talking—now is that wrong?

Yoojin bounces up from his seat and extends his arms wide, as if showing off his wingspan. "You want selca—I mean, picture?" He runs his tongue across his teeth before unleashing his own smile, and the two girls nod vigorously, phones already in hand.

He inserts himself on one side of Min—Gwangju quickly joins, nodding, declaring, "Hello, I love you," which appears to send at least one eye in each girl back toward her skull—both of them Asian-squatting, legs akimbo.

"Jae," one of them calls, but Jae doesn't move.

"Sorry," Min says, "he is sleeping. Airplane, we got here this morning, very sleepy."

"It's okay," the blonder and thinner of the two girls declares, just as her mother says, "You poor things. Let the boy sleep." Between the two of them, they take approximately a hundred photos in blurry succession, but when her friend tilts her camera to try to capture one of Jae sitting head down in his chair, lips splayed and hair limp, Min stands up sharply and darts in front of her, close enough to reach out and touch. "Stay focused," he tells her. "We don't want to bother him, remember?"

Up close, he is only a fistful of inches taller than her and the mothers, but it doesn't matter; he feels like the transfiguration of Jesus, softly lit forehead and body heat and wonder. Four sets of jaws briefly unhinge from their sockets, but slowly, one heavily mascaraed eye blinks after the other in succession.

"We'll delete that one," says her mom, who intuits that even young beautiful men can be slayed by an unflattering candid photo, a uniquely modern condition more transmissible than any disease. She gives her daughter a hard little shove, which the producer, still standing in the middle of the room, takes as his cue to say, "All right, what a treat that was for everyone involved!" Using the padded tips of his fingers again, he shoos the women back into the hallway, where their original silence cracks open and dissolves in a flurry of *omigod-didyouseethat-holyshitfuck-theyaresosexy-imgonnadie*, the aphasic lingo of people who have briefly lost their minds and thus cannot be expected to follow the normal rules of grammar, syntax, or vocabulary.

Right now, they are horny from excitement, doped up on the disbelief of being randomly plucked from the audience and deposited for a precious seven minutes into the orbit of The Band.

But in a month, a week, maybe even a few hours, one of these four women will tire of relieving this moment in her head. Having chewed over to exhaustion every last detail of her singular (not so singular) experience of loving someone who by definition of their job description and existential assignment as *idol* cannot love her back in the kind of highly specific and custom-tailored ways she expects from lesser men, she will start to overanalyze the evidence in damning, less-than-flattering ways. After all, there are two, and only two, options for desire unfulfilled: it will either wither quietly from misuse, its dead parts evaporating back into the atmosphere to be reused and recycled another day for another target, or it will metastasize. There are also two, and only two, kinds of evil in this world: the kind that is born (uninteresting, psychopathic) and the kind that is made. The latter we should all be more terrified of, because it is both predictable (I should've seen it coming, we tell ourselves after the fact) and shocking.

What's going on with Jae? will be the first question and the most generous one after the 212th time the blonder, thinner girl revisits the meet-and-greet in her head. When an assessment of the nonexistent evidence—after all, Min shamed her into deleting that photo of Jae unconscious in his chair—yields no clear answers, she will go onto Quora and Reddit to post this question into the worldwide ether: *Anyone notice The Band does not care as much about their fans anymore?* 2.9K other fans who have not had the pleasure of being within touching distance of the superstars will nevertheless pause their scrolling to comment, in no particular order, on Min's facial expression during The Band's latest televised interview, Asian stoicism or Western stereotyping on full display, or Jae's lack of recent Twitter activity and retweets of fan-generated memes, or the number of months that have passed since Gwangju's last mixtape and Yoojin's last vlog. And, of course, Duri's continued absence, an insult to fans and stans alike whose biases burn solely for him.

Upon seeing the torrent of activity in response to her original question, this once-lucky fan will feel: first, vindicated—*I knew it*, she thinks—then immediately: more suspicious. She will remember Min jumping in front of her, chiding her for the photo. A conspiracy is just a coincidence noticed under conditions of paranoia.

What else is The Band trying to hide? she now asks, first herself, then the rest of the internet. Those who have no idea what she is talking about or recognize the question as that of an unstable person will promptly ignore the query and move on to more rational corners of the web. Those with their own brands of private obsession will recognize a like-minded person when they see one. They will, in long, rambling, and syntactically questionable prose, outline the deep recesses of their imagination. They will take turns annotating each other's revisionist accounts of concerts, posts, sound bites. They will, like the neo-Nazis and flat-Earthers and anti-vaxxers and doomsday cult followers before them, walk away from their devices convinced of their own rationality. They will thereby have created an alternate reality that the rest of us will have to reckon with.

Back in the greenroom, Jae opens one well-lined smokey eye and registers the unfamiliar bust of the new stylist hovering in front of his face, her lemon-sized boobs pointing perkily in his direction as the rest of her squat little body shifts forward and backward, spraying and adjusting before stepping back to assess the situation.

"What time is it?" he says.

The stylist doesn't answer; it's unclear whether he was speaking to her or one of the dozen other people ambling about in the room. She is new. She is even younger than him—twenty-two—a saekki kodi* used to sewing and ironing and assembling jewelry and being harangued by the head "big sister" over hemlines and flyaways but not used to being spoken to by the talent, whose hair she only adjusted because, in his slumber, his bangs had fallen forward asymmetrically across his forehead. To reply when not spoken to is bad, but to ignore when asked a direct and simple question is likely worse, so in

---

*새끼코디 (baby stylist)

a moment of inspiration, she swivels Jae's chair toward the massive countdown clock on the wall. 13:59 to showtime, it says. He jumps.

"Good morning," Gwangju says, walking past him toward the door. "Good afternoon?"

"You missed the meet-and-greet," Min adds. "I saved you from an unflattering photo."

"Wait, what?"

There's no time to unpack or explain; the producer is back, whispering furiously into his mic while pacing with the giddy-up of a sugared-up toddler, and the wang eonni* is already inserting the boys' signature bedazzled earpieces.

When they ascend to the stage, the hysteria is palpable. The host, unused to this level of glee directed at people not herself, especially in the absence of a mass giveaway of freebies, has this funny look on her face: a single eyebrow protrudes into her hairline even as the rest of her expression has been fashioned into a grin, frozen and wide. Three separate times, she opens her mouth to speak long after the boys have sat down, and three separate times, the crowd drowns her out with their utter ignorance of her presence. By now she is merely a nuisance, some means to an end, an unnecessary appendage, an overzealous appendix trying to bring the rest of the body down. After a prolonged series of glances between the members themselves, Min finally raises his finger, a long index one crowned with a thin gold band, and with an obedience typically reserved for dogs, the audience hushes, suddenly cognizant that there's an adult in the room and he wishes to speak.

Before the host can say a thing, Min calls out to the crowd: "We are happy to see you too."

More cheering, clapping, thigh-slapping, several errant whistles from the far corners of the room.

---

*왕언니 (head stylist)

"Now, what are your names again?" The host says this with the kind of impunity familiar to those who've come from a long family tree of colonizers, first from the Old Country, then with the New. At this point, this is the equivalent of meeting Obama and asking him whether it's pronounced *Baa-rock* or *Bar-rake* or something else. After all, The Band has more Twitter followers than both the former president and his successors combined.

The boys look at each other, deciding whether to be amused or offended.

After a beat, Jae says, "I'm the baby."

Yoojin chimes, "I'm the dancer." He points to Gwangju. "Rapper, him—also, Genius."

Min says, "And I would be the one who speaks the most English. You can pretty much just talk to me."

The host, she moves her eyes across each member, squinting and trying to figure out whether it's mockery she's looking at but then remembering that what she is selling here is light and fluffy, a lady comedian in the most digestible format possible. "Well, the real question is whether I'd be able to pronounce your names even if you told me."

A laugh track pumps in from the speakers to supplement the otherwise unamused crowd stunned into silence that this woman could interview the most famous boy band alive and make no effort to conceal her own ignorance. Min confirms, "Our thoughts exactly. We were saving you the trouble." It remains unclear whether he is being generous or sarcastic.

"Now, are those roles you gave yourselves or were they assigned to you?" Then again, no lady comedian makes it this far without being an assassin herself.

Min looks at the camera closest to him and leans forward. "There's this idea in your country that artists are always supposed to be authentic, right? Like that is the vision of the rock star, the rebel, always doing things his own way. He doesn't care what anyone else thinks—"

"Yes, well—"

"No one asks if maybe that itself is an image, an impression that is managed, you understand?" He turns to the woman behind the desk. "As a comedian, you should know, am I right? Even comedians have stage personas they are projecting. You who are here in front of the camera, that is a person you created—"

More squinting: the truth of this revelation would become apparent months later, when a blistering leaked video taken during a staff meeting would reveal just how good of an actress this comedian-host has been this entire time without anyone realizing she was acting, always acting, really.

She looks at her 5x7s. A pause. "Wait, isn't there supposed to be another one of you?" She goes through an exaggerated display of counting, slowly and deliberately, as if set out to prove a point about Americans being terrible at math, especially when there are Asians involved. "Where's number five?"

"Our most handsome member is not here," Min admits. "Normally with him around, we are even more attractive." A collective wave of protest emanates from the audience. When the fandom is not busy questioning their every move, they are busy worrying about each individual band member's self-esteem.

"*They* all seem to think you're very attractive still," the host points out, another compliment-jab. "Look around," she urges. "See anyone you're interested in dating? Would you even date a fan in the first place?"

Min looks at Gwangju, whose jaw muscles shift like ripples underneath almond-milk skin. Yoojin raises a hand well-decorated with thumb rings but without waiting to be called on, says, "Eat, sleep, work. We do only that."

"Come on. That would make you either incredibly boring or an incredible liar."

Jae opens his mouth only to close it again. Min makes a noise that sounds like a laugh, but his eyes suggest he doesn't find the joke funny. "Look, it—"

The host has another thought. "Fine, forget that question. Here's one I think you are allowed to answer: Who is your celebrity crush?"

"American celebrity?"

"Considering you are the only Korean celebrities I know, unless the answer is you would like to date each other, then yes, an American one would be ideal."

Gwangju looks like he is considering, for the first time, what it'd be like to punch a white lady in the cheek on national television: his arms are sitting casually enough on his knees, but his fingers loosen and clench, squeezing and letting go one digit at a time, as if counting the future repercussions of his actions if he were to live a little and finally do what he wants to for once. In twelve hours, this image of him would be a worldwide meme attached to every other irritation known to modern man, but for now the other members look on curiously at his pulsating extremities until finally Jae places an elbow on Gwangju's shoulder and blurts out, "Beyoncé."

"Queen Bey," confirms Min.

"Isn't she a little old for you? Because you all look about twelve."

"Most Americans guess sixteen. We are all actually in our twenties. Some of us close to thirty, even."

"The Queen is ageless," Yoojin inserts.

"Black don't crack, or so I've heard," the host admits. This sounds at least a little racist coming out of her mouth, so The Band says nothing, but to break the awkward silence that follows, Min offers: "If the next question is what American artist we'd like to collaborate with, then our answer is the same: Beyoncé all the way."

A cackle. "Since you boys are so smart, I've got a surprise for you. Hopefully you haven't read my mind on this one." She peers into the audience. The kind of silence you find in horror movies right before blood splatters on the camera lens descends onto the studio. Yoojin's right eyebrow reaches for his left. Jae's arms extend in both directions like a bird readying for flight or a man protecting his precious cargo and fellow comrades. Min glances behind him. Gwangju is still staring at the woman, ready to punish her for whatever's about to happen next.

A flash of polyester flies down the center aisle of the studio audience, then another body zooms by immediately after. In the commotion, even the cameraman captures nothing but blonde ringlets and sequins followed by a tuft of sherpa and a spray of cocoa hair rushing the stage. It's hard to see behind the tactical masks each moving object has on. Before either woman—girl? boy? humanoid?—makes it to the elevated platform where the guests have been sitting on cloud sofas and the host has been ejecting one-liners disguised as questions behind the world's largest desk, two more shadows appear from stage left. They're packing the kind of exaggerated accessory found in Saturday morning cartoons: rifles painted in obnoxious shades of citrus (neon green, highlighter orange), mounted with football-shaped dispensers of ammo. Two hundred pairs of audience heads swivel toward the armed duo now storming the stage, forcing The Band themselves to turn from one impending threat to behold another.

Min's eyes grow as the rest of his face shrivels; for this brief horrific moment in time, his features finally take on the exaggerated neotenic anime proportions the Asian world find so damn attractive. Jae throws himself on Yoojin's lap, limbs everywhere, hair displaced in all the wrong directions. Only Gwangju appears stuck. For all their worldly experience, these boys have never played paintball and do not know what its paraphernalia look like. What they do know is what everyone else in the world knows: America is a land so free—or perhaps so addicted to the idea of freedom—that its people can gun each other down in broad daylight with weapons they can find at the same place a man can get condoms. Classrooms, discount stores, concerts, garlic festivals, parades, discotheques, massage parlors—America does not discriminate about where a citizen can exert his God-given right to bear arms.

By the time the initial green bullet stuns the first body rushing the stage with its rather erotic-looking splatter across an otherwise well-protected face, Yoojin is already on the floor, Jae having taken over his spot on the couch. A hiss and slap later, the other target is also down, sitting on all fours on the ground beneath the stage, tangerine paint dripping on her perfect denim jacket, having missed her headgear by an inch south. Min uncurls himself in time to see her crab-walk backward toward the exit doors. Behind him, the two snipers give a teensy curtsy, followed by a kind of anachronistic bow historically reserved for greeting heads of state before walking backward into the curtains. A nervous giggle escapes from the front row; the small-limbed tweens stare at their fellow fan incapacitated in the aisle. Doused in green liquid latex and limping a little, she is retreating in animal fashion the same way she came, on all fours, dripping in jewelry and goo. Can anything be more sexually perverse than this? They shake their heads but convulse their shoulders at the same time. Maybe this is what the adults mean when they say "slapstick humor."

The giggle is contagious, the host herself the super-spreader at the epicenter: she shakes uncontrollably behind that great big desk of hers, so amused she is. The audience gives in to the pressure to laugh before Min, at last, condones whatever the fuck just happened with his own snort, and Yoojin, having been helped off the floor by Jae, offers the camera a stunned little smile.

"Ever play paintball?" the woman asks. When no one attempts to answer her question, she offers, "If you can't date them, the least you can do is let them fight over you. Your fans have always been notorious for the lengths they'd go to for you."

"We would like to play with you." Gwangju enunciates every last syllable; there is no hiding his meaning. "This paint ball. We play now?"

The audience, they think this is a great idea. The laughter cata-lyzes into cheering, which quickly devolves into chanting "Paint! Ball! Paint! Ball!" with the exact same kind of syncopated rhythm middle schoolers everywhere recognize from after-school fights when two kids circle one another while the rest of the crowd croaks, "Fight! Fight! Fight!"

Gwangju stands, placing his decorative Harry Potter eyeglasses carefully on the dent left behind on the couch. The other members peer up at him, and suddenly they look small, a little uncertain, but the Genius looks like Daddy, who comes to rectify situations when the kids are no longer all right. When he takes off his vest, the cheers get louder, shriller; a girl can sexualize anything if her mind is in the right place, even a sleeveless Argyle sweater defanged with buttons, and the host, she looks up at him too, but all her orifices are pucker-ing at the same time: eyes, nose, that anus of a mouth.

"Now, now," she says, but no one can hear her, and for the first time since becoming too famous to fail, she looks a little afraid.

"We don't have enough equipment." She says this to Min, who is not looking in her direction at all, his eyes still stuck on the only person in the room still standing. Even the cameramen are back to squatting over their itsy black stools.

"You and me, then," Gwangju replies, suddenly very proficient in English. "Two guns, two masks." He holds out his thumb and index finger. Is he signaling the number two in Korean or calling her a loser, American style? We will never know.

"Commercial break!" she cries. Without waiting for the cameras to cut away, she jumps up and extends her open palms, grabbing Min's hand, then Jae's, with a vigor she has not had to expend for a very long time. She walks around the table to shake Yoojin's hand too before finally turning to Gwangju and putting her hand firmly against his back. She reaches around for one of her trademark bear hugs. "This is my fucking show, don't you forget it." Her mouth is ajar as she murmurs this, lips contorted into her trademark grin. Who knew that she could've been a ventriloquist in a separate life?

Afterward, back in the Escalade, Jae inquires: "What would've happened if they missed and hit an unprotected audience member?"

"Or us?" adds Yoojin.

"I think," says Gwangju, "that was supposed to be funny."

The members all look at him for signs of fury. "Were you joking or serious when you essentially challenged the host to a duel on national television?" Min wants to know; the number one job of a leader is to figure out what your constituents are capable of.

"Americans and their guns," the Genius says instead. "For a country that has more mass shootings a year than there are days, it's funny that blasting each other with painted guns and bullets is considered an actual game."

"Maybe they're always practicing," Jae offers. "So that they're prepared for the worst."

"I doubt you can prepare for tragedy," Gwangju surmises. "If we could, we'd all live longer."

Sometimes geniuses can predict the future, but they still can't change it.

Gwangju, of course, is not the only genius in this story. Back in Seoul, in Gangnam-gu, Pinocchio is doing zoomies around his L-shaped desk while his secretary guards his door and counts the number of concentric circles he has made.

"As they say, all publicity is good publicity," she offers, after having reached double digits.

"No one says that but Americans," he wails.

"Exactly," she reminds him. "And they are in America, no?"

Pinocchio pauses his speed walking, surprised that a woman whose sole job is to follow directions may also secretly (not so secretly?) be an empress of logic. The revelation is a little unnerving; he wonders what other cards she has to play. In a bout of paranoia, he considers the possibility that she is the true genius here, and he a mere savant, learned but deficient. Easier to take yourself down a couple of notches than let someone else do the honors, he decides: "You are blaming me for sending them there, and for that, I do not blame you." The mental jiujitsu of turning words of affirmation and encouragement into indictments and character assassination must be a uniquely Asian skill set they teach little boys and girls in the Far East right after filial piety and multiplication tables.

"The comedienne—" the secretary says. "What is her last name?"

"How am I supposed to know?" Pinocchio has gone back to wailing. "Her talk show, it goes only by her first name. I bet you no one even—"

"Exactly," she repeats. "She is a troll without even a family name, at least one we know about. Why do you care what she thinks?"

But Pinocchio is not as inhuman as some of his decisions suggest. "You think this is about—" He refuses to call the American celebrity host by name, not unlike the way a former president declined to name his famous intern, and instead also opts to refer to her as "That Woman." He shakes his head. "This is about my—the—boys. With Duri gone, The Band is probably one crisis away from early retirement. This is not the hill I want them to die on."

"You want them to die on a different hill?"

Pinocchio looks surprised for the second time in a single afternoon. "I want them to live forever," he tells her. It is the most obvious thing in the world, he thinks.

13

Antis (D-2)

Remember: the fan, now stan, from the meet-and-greet was also in the talk show audience. She has a name, but the unwell deserve protection too, perhaps even more so than the psychologically hearty (who are better at taking care of themselves), so let's call her Sasa, short for *sasaeng*, of course. She left her seat in the studio audience with the strange feeling of having been part of something that never fully materialized or met its total potential, like a miscarriage parading as a particularly heavy period. The abortive six minutes in the greenroom was just the start. The interview, cut short by a practical joke that neither translated nor landed, made even her mother turn to her afterward and inquire: "Wait, that's it? What about the album? What about Duri?" Not to mention the prized nomination for the historically prestigious but recently controversial award well-known for recognizing tokens but never letting them win. Sasa only frowned, shrugging, because the real question was: Who is to blame?

The internet is terribly good at many things, including that it allows mere mortals to travel at the speed of light. Or at least at the speed of 5G, which is close.

Shortly after Thursday midnight rolls into Friday morn, after a prolonged and unproductive stint looking at erotic selfies on Instagram by otherworldly females sent here from alien planets to make ordinary women feel bad, Sasa goes back to her latest discussion thread about *The Band not caring about their fans anymore* and *The Band hiding something*. She discovers she has hit a nerve, which apparently is not that hard to do when you shoot a gun into the dark room that is the World Wide Web already brimming with bodies. The conversation has spiraled to subsume not just her initial discussion, but in subsequent subreddits and Twitter, threads about each individual Band member and their arguable moral failures. What starts as a reinvigorated debate over Duri's now infamous song about Japanese fathers eating their Korean sons has now devolved into a much broader list of alleged atrocities.

Yoojin refused to take a photo with a restaurant hostess who requested nicely during one of their travel video blogs. Gwangju mispronounced the name of a famous British-crooner-turned-American-pop-sensation during a radio interview ("Ahnah," he said, the way the Spanish say it, as opposed to the more Anglicized "Ehnah," which listeners went to great lengths to remind him). Jae looked puffy after an awards show thanks to a long, gluttonous night of drinking (or so people presumed). The maknae line talked too much about their diets. The hyung line failed to release a PSA about eating disorders. Duri disappeared without informing the fanbase of the precise dates of his departure, return, and purpose of travel. The Band collectively donated a cool million to the GoFundMe account of a recently slain activist moonlighting as a fellow rapper but then collectively opted to keep the rest of their billions.

A little after one a.m., she sends this out to her digital living room: *Let's send them a message. Remind them who we fans are. They need us more than we need them.*

Which, in retweets and reposts, turns into simply: *Let's teach them a lesson.* Even virtual telephones warble.

When she tags Rockefeller Center, #48thStreetSide, #standby, #audience, #TheBand, along with the logo of the live comedy sketch show featuring them as their musical act on Saturday, even the middle-school stans can decode her invitation.

The first two people in the standby ticket line show up three hours before twilight, after school's been let out but before the tourists have descended onto Rockefeller Plaza for a different kind of Friday night lights. A girl arrives with her best friend from homeroom. The two of them refer to themselves as OGs—they discovered The Band in the early days during one of their routine summers in Seoul to visit their ajummas and get their eyelids stitched before their eighth-grade graduation.

Fast-forward five years and here they are now, about to be freshmen at one of the lesser-known universities in the city (not Columbia, not NYU), still carrying around their first loves but with the distinct dissatisfactory feeling that things are not the same. Over time, the songs have gotten more love-songy, but these girls have gotten more jaded. They miss the hard edge in the boys' voices as they rapped about the dangers of filial piety and being good but not interesting; they don't get Duri's heady lyrics full of metaphors, and they do not enjoy feeling stupid. They are too American and woke to care about #chinilpa,* but they also do not appreciate cannibalism in song lyrics, no matter how figurative and avant-garde. The lesson these two want to teach The Band is how to travel backward in time.

A coven of six middle schoolers shows up armed with fake IDs, all proclaiming that they were born at least four to five years before their actual dates of birth. Their various shades of black clothing

---

*Originally used to refer to Koreans who helped Japan during their colonial rule, but now used to insult Koreans seen as too pro-Japanese.

match their strikingly unanimous shades of white skin, as if today is Halloween and together they are the yin to each other's yang. They say nothing to the OGs in front of them and even do not talk to each other, but rather opt to stare collectively at each of their respective phone screens and only occasionally giggle before showing another person what exactly is so terribly funny. As recent converts to The Band-dom, they have few concrete complaints but a shared love of punishment, retribution, all that jazz. If you remember middle school, you are not surprised by any of this.

When they unzip their puffy jackets and fuzzy coats, the iron-on block letters from homemade sweatshirts peek out: half of them have _ANCEL, the other half, _URI. Nobody is illiterate; anyone can put the two together and figure out the missing letters.

Sasa arrives. She wastes no time and situates herself between the two groups of girls, making no effort to observe the laws of forming a proper line. "You all here for The Band?" Then, "Nice shirts."

Without counting their nods, she moves on, holding out her screen: "I started the original post calling everyone here, but let me just say right now: I'm not an anti-fan. No, really, I'm not, I love my boys, we don't deserve them, really, we don't, but I'm not gonna lie, I'm a little disappointed in them right now—"

No one inquired, but one of the OGs says anyway, "They sold out, if you ask me."

To which one of the younger girls replies, "It's Cancel Time."

"They've all done something, that's for sure, yep. They take the fandom for granted now, I think, and don't get me started on that song called 'The Hole', I don't even . . ." The line lengthens as brandishes her phone around, moths drawn to the device's light: a mixed-gender clump of garishly dressed undergraduates advertising the school colors of their respective state universities; two more groups of tweens, identifiable by their metallic braces and chromatic lip gloss.

"Look, my idea is this, hear me out and pass it down. I'm gonna post the instructions online too, so make sure you're following me. We are the audience, our power lies in our hands, like literally, they want us there to clap, monkey, clap, but I am not a monkey, no, and you are not a monkey, are you? So, when the lights dim and The Band comes on, remember: no clapping, no screaming, got it? We don't clap when they come on and we don't clap when they finish, not for the first song, not for the second. It's a live studio audience; they won't have time to react or find a new one or pump in a fake clap track, so it's brilliant. We're gonna give them the silent treatment. My momma uses it, and my grand momma before her. I don't know what the feminists would say about it, but let me say this: women have been using it for a hundred thousand years, and if worked for them then, you better believe it's gonna work for us."

The more Sasa talks, the more her voice trails into a slow drawl, like a woman returning to her Confederate roots.

Over the course of the next dozen hours, her message gets repeated and passed down between conglomerates of lawn chairs and sleeping bags and tarp. If there are fans there who did not show up to boycott or communicate any passive-aggressive messages to The Band, they do not say anything. In the face of a furious woman, it's best to keep quiet and carry on. Sasa herself becomes a bit of a temporary celebrity. Her follower count doubles by midnight, and by the time the studio pages emerge at seven a.m. to dole out the coveted white placeholder cards, if she had doubters to begin with, they have all switched sides, thoroughly convinced that tough love is a moral imperative akin to Christianity during the Middle Ages or Democracy in the twentieth century—ideals for which there are no alternatives.

When the incident makes the news rounds on Sunday morning, psychologists are the only ones not surprised. Studies show that a collection of people is the single most powerful thing in the world. A person will do just about anything to belong to a group.

14

Conditions Without Cures (D-1)

D uri, Duri. I'd watched The Band's uncomfortable appearance on the Friday afternoon talk show take the unexpectedly violent turn while Duri took another one of his naps, an apparently addictive habit that he either had all along or developed at my house during the past three days.

But on Saturday night, we are both on the same uncomfortably modern couch in my living room, stark angles enshrouded in white Italian leather and spindly frames, staring at the oversized Samsung screen fastened to the wall. Luc and the kids, meanwhile, are in the den with the comfy but ugly seating in overstuffed and stain-resistant microfiber, watching an old American TV (Philips Magnavox) play an even older American tradition (weekend football). To commemorate this special occasion, I've made cookies from a box. Duri doesn't even look at them, but I've not managed to stop depositing them into my mouth.

"Want me to translate anything?" I ask him, coming up for air mid-bite.

He makes a little noise, a half-baked thing between a laugh and a cough. "Now you speak Korean?"

"What I mean is, want me to explain anything about the show or these sketches they've got on? I'm not sure if the humor translates."

"I don't care. Only The Band, I watch."

"You have that app still."

He waves his hand before dropping it in his lap, the global gesture for *fuck it.*

"Want a beer?" I ask instead.

"Ei, you drink beer?"

"I *have* beer. That's the important part. Luc's the one that drinks it. But I will play along if you wish."

"Bud Light?"

"I didn't say we drank American beer. I think you might've just racially profiled my white husband. We've got Coronas. Heinekens, too, maybe. Of course, also the hard stuff. Rum and Coca-Cola, I mean. An old bottle of vodka too. I may not drink myself but I will make Jell-O shots for a party."

Duri frowns. "I drink anything. I can drink a lot."

Now it is my turn to frown. "Do you have a problem?"

"Problem?"

"You know." I splay myself across the couch, extending thumb and pinky to approximate the length of a beer bottle. "Are you an alcoholic is what I mean."

Duri makes the same hybrid sound of cough meets laugh. "What you mean, alcoholic? Koreans drink. We go to work, we drink after. Sometimes, all night. Men, sometimes they fall sleep on the street, too much to drink. But then they wake up and go back to work, no problem."

"A functional alcoholic is what that sounds like."

"Don't worry," he says again, fully knowing that if worry was something people could turn on and off, half of my field would be out of a job.

"I'm not worried"—a lie; worrying is one of the few talents I have left that shows no signs of slowing down—"I'm just saying: Can you stop drinking if you want to?"

"Why I want to stop drinking?"

"To prove that you can! What's the Korean word for addiction?"

"Americans, addicted to cookies and wearing shorts," he says, eyeing me.

"You calling me fat?" It would not be the first time an Asian person implied this, and for this reason alone, I married white. "Or a slutty dresser?" After all, I've got on the kind of shorts with lettering across the back (never mind what it says) that demands to be read, then promptly judged. Duri does not bother to confirm or deny: "It's not a competition," I tell him, defensive over what, I cannot tell you. As retribution, I do not retrieve any beer, American or otherwise.

"Just watch," he replies, already having moved on. Tonight's host—a brunette actress ethnically ambiguous enough to get away with starring in an egregiously long series of kung fu movies—is grinning on the screen and making small talk with the show's own band, an ethnically varied group of men whose primary purpose seems to be meeting the studio's diversity quota. The band leader, he is volleying softballs, mostly noises in the affirmative while the host muses on the presumed army of fangirls in the audience.

"They've been camped out here for days," she tells him, as if this is news to anyone. "It's amazing that they look as nice as they do, considering their fairly recent bout of sleeping outdoors on the sidewalk."

"Girls, they clean up nice," the band leader affirms, already laughing because he is eager to keep his job.

"Now, this band, The Band. You heard of them?"

"Who hasn't?"

"I only found out about them yesterday." It's unclear whether this is a joke, but the band man leans forward and grips his mic, so convulsive is his well-rehearsed guffawing.

"This woman, she comedienne?" inquires Duri.

"No, an actor," I tell him. "From those martial arts movies."

"This is funny?" he presses.

"Not yet."

When the music starts and Min is the first to bounce out, all hair and jeans, followed by the rest of the boys, each one wearing a form of denim more aggressively distressed than the last, I look at Duri, whose face is as unreadable as the ancient stereotypes say.* Throughout the performance, his body is draped across the inhospitable loveseat like an oversized throw—feet and arms hanging over opposing armrests, knees apart at an obtuse angle—but his expression does not budge, as if frozen on Zoom. Only when the melody stops at the song's last high note and The Band members unfurl themselves into their final resting positions do we notice something is not going to plan.

"Shh-shhi-shhi-bal." He points at the screen, both hands extended, zombie-like and accusatory. The camera shot sits on the boys, hunched over like petals in the middle of the stage, waiting for the applause to be their cue to stand and bow, but no applause comes. A second, a beat—Jae finally lifts his chin up to peer back at the audience, and the camera angle follows his gaze, but all we see are rows of girls, their faces shrouded and unreadable in the dark lighting of the studio, arms crossed, not a single one of them clapping. As the camera continues to pan, it hesitates briefly when it reaches the back row, where a half dozen white shirts glow in the dark, their hand-drawn lettering stark and loud. CANCEL CANCEL CANCEL DURI DURI DURI, it spells out. It's unclear whether these girls meant to stutter in their messaging.

By the time Min stands up and bows to the silent audience, his dignity his prize, Duri has thrown himself back on the couch, hugging an armrest.

"It's a prank, I think." And by "I think," I mean I am praying to a God I no longer believe in except in moments when there is no one

*See: the "inscrutable Asian."

to blame and everything to lose. Duri doesn't hear me, or doesn't understand, or thinks I'm sort of a harmless idiot. His hands hover over his ears like some kind of weird superhero whose primary power lies in their ability to mess with people's heads.

When the theme song for the show starts emanating from the screen, Duri can't help but peek in time to catch a glimpse of the members retreating—and when he does, the convulsions begin, first slow and rumbly like an aftershock but then progressively more animated, his shoulders contracting and releasing so many times in a row I wonder if he's exercising. The noises that escape—first from his nostrils, then somewhere in the back of the throat—sound neither human nor animal, but primordial, like soup, something that precedes sentience.

It's my turn to stand up. "Are you—?" "All right" is the wrong term to use here. I'm not okay, he's not okay, no one has been okay since Eve ate that damn piece of fruit and we've been paying for it ever since. "Laughing or crying?" I decide. "Or something else?"

Duri's face makes its way toward mine. His eyes are pinched closed like the seams of a dumpling, but his mouth is free and so extended I can see a silver crown sitting on a molar. At the risk of being shoved for my impending violation or being perceived as an aspiring adulteress—it's unclear which one would be worse—I cup his ears for him if for no other purpose but to hold him still in case he really is having a seizure, and when I do, his lids fly open, but he is not staring back at me,* only the screen where his own phantom limbs are splayed across a different couch, a promotional still shot of

---

*I realize then that I've finally reached the age of invisibility, the point of no return, when a woman is no longer perceived as a woman and therefore can cross all kinds of lines egregiously, can flirt with whomever, however, whenever, can touch a man, even a beautiful one, wherever I please and nothing bad can or will happen because I am no longer a potential ride, to be broken or domesticated or taken home. I am just another horse. Who's ever been offended by a horse?

The Band in its previous five-member condition. Only then do I notice that even in the photo, Gwangju is giving the camera the look of death and Yoojin looks like a migrant child lost between worlds and Jae is peering straight into the lens, as if experimenting with telepathy, and Min has his hands on each knee, sitting erect and resembling an Asian grandpa, having suddenly aged.

"Hajimaa," Duri yells.

I release him, assuming he is talking to me, but to our surprise he places my hands back over each ear, only to resume the convulsing.

"You are making me nervous. You know that, right?"

The father of psychology—William James was his name—had this theory that no one actually knows what they're really feeling at the time they're feeling something. The way he saw it, feelings were just the stories we told ourselves to account for our own behaviors. We see a bear, we run, and as we are fleeing, we look down, noticing our flight and beating heart and perpendicular neck hairs, and go, *that's fear*. The body reacts first, and the brain catches up after the fact to do the explaining.

A century later, two guys—they were always guys—came up with a neat trick to prove that James was right, more or less: They got an attractive woman named Gloria to show up at a tourist trap in Vancouver, one that locals (derisively) and visitors (gleefully) alike referred to as the Indiana Jones Bridge. It's a massive contraption of creaky wooden planks conjoined by steel ropes that sway above a two-hundred-plus-foot drop, interrupted only by a bed of rocks on the bottom. She got on one end and waited for the single guys to show up. When they did, she approached them one by one, asking them to fill out a survey and handing over her phone number in the name of science. Later, she did the same thing over a smaller, safer bridge, one that neither moved nor threatened anyone's life. In the days that followed, Gloria counted her calls and discovered more men dialed her from the dangerous bridge than the safe one. It turns out, William James was right: these men could not identify the true cause of their racing hearts or butterflies or sweaty hands and assumed that it was Gloria, not the bridge, that made them react so.*

If it was true of a bunch of guys in Vancouver, it might be true of Duri: the boy himself has no idea if he is laughing or crying, if what we just saw was a protest or a form of cruelty distilled into its most digestible format (comedy). Whatever it was, it seems to have pressed some button inside him. By the time his shaking turns into hiccups and the hiccups taper off to a long-aggravated sigh, Duri retrieves his phone from his pocket and with a warning swipe, starts talking.

"They're never going to get over this. Min, Jae, Yoojin, definitely not Gwangju, you can see it in his face. People never get over anything, seven years with the same group of guys doing everything together has taught me this, the five of us as different as can be, but this we have in common: we get over nothing. There are things you don't recover from, not because you cannot but because what is the fun of it, always moving on to the next thing?"

He continues, "My father, he treats life like this one long race to the finish line. Since he was eighteen, he has been this this way, always trying to find the thing that works and doing it over and over again until it breaks or dies or stops working, whichever comes first. Do not worry, he is alive, and do not worry, my mother and brother are not dead either, no one is dead, they are too busy working, working away, my father at the same company he joined since he graduated college and my mother at the same house I was born into. They hate each other. That is why, you see, work is a balm. Tiger Balm, you know it?"

"I'm Asian, of course I know—"

"Even my brother and me, we can love each other now because we are too busy working to see each other, maybe just once a year, that is

---

*See: Dutton and Aron 1974.

all we need, all we care to do, any more than that and we will be back
to hating each other—"

"You hate your brother?"

"Do you hear me? I love my brother. I said I used to hate him when
I was young, but not now, now I cannot even hate him if I try. I do not
see him enough to hate him."

"Is there a reason you're spending your"—I don't know what to
call this, whatever the hell Duri is doing—"this break, time off, whatever, here instead of at home in Korea with your family?"

This, Duri finds funny, so very hilarious. There's no mistaking his
quaking shoulders now. He is straight-up cackling. "You funny guy,"
he says in English.

"I'm not joking. Explain it to me, please."

Duri elaborates into his device. "My parents, they got this dog after
I left for college—this was before I joined The Band—and the dog, he
is not a good one, there is something wrong with him. Very unusual in
Korea for this to happen, we have a better breeding program than you
Americans do with your many pounds and animal shelters. But this
dog, something must have happened to him in a previous life because
the first weekend he is home, my father, he has these meat bones in
his pocket that he brought home for the puppy, and the puppy wants
them, and he gives one to him, but the puppy wants another one,
and he says no, but then the puppy tries to chew on his pocket, so he
pushes it away, but the puppy is mad. He bites my father on his hand,
pierces his palm straight through like Jesus on the cross, and my father smacks him with his other hand, but the puppy just bites down
on his forearm instead. There is blood everywhere, my father is yelling, my brother is not home." Duri pauses, looks at me. "Do you know
what my mother is doing when this is happening?"

"I don't know, calling 911—the Korean version, I mean—the police?"

"You are almost right. This is why you are married with a husband and I am here in your house single forever. Because my mother,

she is on the phone, but she is not calling the police—119 is what we dial, the opposite numbers, no one is creative enough to come up with anything new anymore—she is calling the store. The store where they bought the puppy. She is screaming at the shop owner, demanding a refund for this useless dog, threatening to warn all of Seoul about them, while my father is trying to get the animal to let go of his arm and bleeding all over the carpet, and when the dog finally gives up and my dad goes to the sink to rinse out the wound and use a dish towel to slow the bleeding, he turns to my mother and tells her to hang up and call 119, but she will not do it. You know why?"

"Your mother sounds like a—" But there are certain things no one is allowed to call someone else's mother. Some four-letter words can only be served by blood relatives.

"Because the store owner is coming over to retrieve the dog, she does not want to miss it and have to reschedule. She definitely does not want the thing one more minute in her apartment. Meanwhile my dad is leaning on the kitchen counter bleeding out, and he tells her, 'If I pass out on this floor, you will not be able to get me to the car in order to take me to the doctor,' and does she really want the fire brigade coming up there to haul his body to the hospital and seeing the blood everywhere?"

"Your dad sounds like a practical man. Is he really the guy your song is based on? Is he—" But to say "Japanese" at this point seems like the equivalent of asking *What are you?* Every Asian's least-favorite question to be asked.

Duri ignores the instigation and says instead, "Being practical: It is our birthright as Asians, is it not? You are Chinese, your people invented gunpowder, agriculture, noodles and left biology and physics and chemistry to the ancient Greeks. My point is, my mother, she saw my father bleeding to death and her first, second, and third reaction was to call the store. She is not a bad person, but this is who they are, they are never going to change, and my father, he does not even feel bad about this. I asked him after my brother told me the story, 'Did you and Mother have a fight afterward?' And he said, 'What is there to fight about? Your mother listened to me in the end, and we went to the hospital, and now we do not have a dog anymore.' Do you see what I mean? Finish line, that is what he cares about. He wants to die in that house without a list of problems, without problematic sons. The path of least resistance."

"Is that why you're here? The path of least resistance?"

At this, Duri smiles, the first I've seen since his arrival, and his eyes trail down the length of my torso as if considering it seriously for the first time, but this moment manages to be both spectacular and sad. "You are married woman," he says, back in English. "Also, noona."

"Exactly. I am older than you with a forgiving white husband, two kids, a full-time job that doesn't require me to leave the house, and a rudimentary understanding of Korean. Which is great, because Dispatch doesn't touch civilians, particularly non-Korean ones, and TMZ never comes this far away from the 405 freeway. My husband doesn't really know who you are, and more importantly, does not care. For reasons that are probably a little racist in origin, he has never managed to find an Asian man threatening, not even my own father when he told him no, he can't have his blessing to marry me. Not one but two kids means I'm not about to do anything reckless. The cushy job of an academic means I'm financially comfortable with enough free time to still keep you company. Am I seducing you yet with my low expectations?"

Duri says nothing, just holds that devastating little grin. "You psychologist," he adds. "You read mind?"

"Yes, and you should be ashamed of yourself." But I can't help smiling a little too.

15

Take Me to Church (D-Day)

It's Sunday morning. I am already at church, repenting for my sins, past and future. The pastor, a tall cowboy and verified local celebrity—a chaebol, Duri would call him, after one glance at his excessively nice shoes—is lubing us up with a long clean joke to make whatever he really wants to tell us more digestible. The theme for the current sermon series is "It's the End of the World and the ___ Are Winning." Two weeks prior, it was the Antichrists. Who knew it was always meant to be plural? Apparently, the Antichrist is less of a specific person (Luc, a lifelong Republican, briefly thought it was Obama before Trump came along and wiped out the competition) and more of a spirit, one that is prone to infiltrate your news feed and social media accounts and governing bodies, so watch out.

Then last week, it was the False Prophets. Pastor Brett didn't name any names, but we all knew he was talking about those other guys at bigger, shinier congregations who make the news every few cycles. It's never a good sign when a church leader lands himself in *Vanity Fair* or even *Christianity Today*. It is almost always an affair or something worse. I have it on good authority that a bunch of us in the pews had read their *New York Times*–bestselling books and purchased entire albums of their worship music on iTunes and downloaded their podcasts and, if we were real shameless in our walks with the Lord, even caught glimpses of them leading well-preserved blondes to Jesus on *The Real Housewives of Orange County*.

Then came the articles. The Bible says sin is sin, but try convincing the Church of that. We forgive anybody except the guy behind the pulpit. Him we hold responsible for the relationship with the Instagram darling he was trying to save and the three-figure haircuts and four-figure watches and the string of massage parlors registered under his name and the long line of hired help from godforsaken countries he brought home and did God knows what with.

When the celebrities photoed getting baptized by him almost go blind from relapses and speedy overdoses, we go to him for an accounting. A shepherd must keep track of his sheep. When another Famous Person stops showing up to his Sunday services and stops retweeting his midweek inspirational messages, we wonder what that person knows. When we show up to our own churches on the Lord's Day, heavy from a week's worth of unwanted news, we are primed and pumped to say *Mm-hmm, Amen* when our own exceedingly attractive pastor calls out his brethren for what men in power have been doing ever since Lot pimped out his daughters or Abraham took advantage of his slave girl Hagar.

This week, Pastor Brett has changed his tune. This week, it's Jesus. Syntactically, this does not work well for his fill-in-the-blank sermon ("It's the end of the world and the Jesus are winning"), but no one ever claimed that good grammar was next to godliness. For a guy who lost his firstborn child a year prior, he is astoundingly optimistic today. You're thinking it; I'll say it: it just seems a little blasphemous. God gives you hope, but no one ever claimed He made you happy. Those who don't learn this early on—it's in the fine print—will invariably not be Christians for long. The key to a long relationship with Jesus is tempered expectations.

Brett—we are tempted to drop the *Pastor* title whenever he exceeds our expectations, an almost always unpleasant occurrence—is high on either the Holy Spirit or a new set of antidepressants today. Jesus is winning, he tells us. Indeed, Jesus has already won, despite all evidence to the contrary. As he told the teachers of the law, the kingdom of heaven is here among us. Does God lie? We shake our heads no but think: *God has some explaining to do.*

Afterward, over donut holes in the lobby, Luc tells Duri, "You know our pastor's kid died last year?" It is unclear what prompted this or why my husband feels the need to pass along news of the tragedy. Then, to me: "You know that's the third pastor we know that's buried their own child?"

"Lars—the Harvard guy, from Christ Community—his was a miscarriage. That counts?" I ask.

"Stillbirth. His wife was like eight months pregnant. How can you not remember? She wouldn't come back to church for like a year."

"We weren't there when it happened. We were only there for the aftermath. Although it was all anyone could talk about."

"And before him, in Cambridge, was Dan, from Santa Barbara. His daughter—she was named after a fruit or a vegetable—what was her name? Gone at seven from leukemia after battling it since birth."

"Peaches? Clementine?"

"It wasn't Peaches for fuck's sake."

"We're in church, honey."

"Let's not blaspheme a dead pastor's kid by suggesting he gave her a name I like to save for exotic dancers."

"This guy, what happened to his baby?" Duri interrupts. Sometimes all it takes is a third party to preclude a fight.

"COVID," says Luc. "Right when we all thought the pandemic was over officially, can you believe it? It was around the time when everyone was getting their latest round of boosters. Mae and I, we were vaccinated ourselves, all the adults we knew had gotten theirs already. Boosters for babies weren't even a thing yet. One day his daughter comes down with a cold she can't shake. Three weeks later, she takes a nap she never gets up from."

"You need to stop calling it a cold. It was obviously not a cold," I remind him.

"He knows what I mean." We both look at Duri for confirmation.

"Wa, why he so happy, then?" he asks.

"That's what I was thinking!" It's hard not to be giddy as I say this. Finally, someone to share my doubt with.

"Jesus Christ, have you been listening to the sermon at all? Are you even a Christian?" Luc demands. "You ever heard of this thing called hope?"

"It's been a year of fire and brimstone, end times, Revelations, the furious and jealous God of the Old Testament. I'm just saying, the sudden turn is a little jarring. Something happen between last Sunday and this Sunday that we don't know about?"

"Zoloft," Duri offers.

"Excuse me?" Luc has the same look on his face he gives pedestrians when they walk into the middle of the street like they're looking for a new way to die.

"Lexapro, Celexa, Paxil. Or Prozac, original classic."

"You know your antidepressants." It feels wrong that I am a little impressed by this.

"Pastor Brett is not taking anything," Luc says.

"How do you know?" I ask.

"I know."

"Have you asked him? Are you buddies on a first-name basis now? Does he even know who we are?"

Luc shakes his head. "He would have no business being on that stage if he were."

"What, it's Jesus take the wheel or nothing? We're not Christian Scientists. God doesn't have anything against medication."

"Does he, though? We're not talking Tylenol or penicillin here."

"Doesn't matter. The mind is part of the body. The 'mental' in mental illness just refers to the symptoms. The causes for all sickness are the same. Something inside you breaks, and if you don't fix it, it just might kill you." This, I teach every semester in Psychopathology, if for no other reason than to show undergrads eager to self-diagnose their own troubles that knowing the etiology of mental illness may be the only comfort we're allowed given how bad we are at actually curing it.

"If you're so sure the pastor's on meds, why don't you go right up to him and ask the man? He's still shaking hands by the double doors," Luc declares.

"Don't be a buddy-fucker," I remind my husband. "I will do no such thing."

"I go ask," says Duri, his second offer in a single morning.

Before either Luc or I can process those three syllables, Duri is already standing in line behind the last remaining parishioners, hands folded in front of his crotch like a patient schoolboy.

"Is he doing this for you?" Luc is not the jealous type, but he sounds strangely suspicious.

"I could say he's doing this for you. You're the one who suggested it."

"We're not going to be able to come back here next Sunday, you know that, right?"

"If he does what he said he'll do, we're never gonna be able to come back here again."

"If we leave now, maybe no one will ever know."

"Too late." Duri, now at the head of the line, is pointing at us and smiling. Brett glances briefly in our direction but either does not recognize us or does not care, so well trained is he on focusing all his glorious attention on the singular person talking and nothing else—a gift pastors everywhere seem to have, to the great chagrin of their wives.

For a guy whose English is his second language and who seems to constantly need a live translation app to have a conversation with me, Duri appears to have no trouble talking now. Maybe he's pretending, but at every pause, Brett is nodding vigorously, his forehead totally clear of fork tines suggestive of excessive mental effort at understanding what the hell this guy is saying. Is this the Holy Spirit at work? If I were a better Christian, or perhaps just a more charismatic one, I'd be inclined to believe that at least one of these men has just been bestowed with the gift of tongues. The only alleged case of such gifts that I've ever seen was when my own mother started stuttering consonants in rapid succession during one of her particularly animated prayers—*de de de de*, she'd say, tongue clicking furiously against the roof of her mouth, as if petitioning for escape. I'd always assumed that whatever she was muttering was some made-up language meant to take up space and remind God to keep on listening, but apparently, she'd been speaking Korean all along. She was just saying *yes yes yes yes*, which is exactly what Duri said last night in his own mother tongue when he, too, cried *de de de de*, albeit in a totally different context where neither of us was thinking about the Holy Spirit.

"Shit, they're walking over," says Luc.

Brett strides ahead of Duri and grabs Luc by the hand. "My brother," he says, the universal euphemism for *remind me of your name*.

"Luc." My husband, ever the mind-reader. "We met when you were still a youth pastor back at Calvary Chapel and I was still an atheist."

Brett nods his head, unfazed by the news. "Now look at us!" Without asking my name or relation, he goes on to ask: "Did you know your guest here recently won a Grammy?"

Duri shrugs, a little embarrassed. "They know, they know."

"I care less about him and more about you," Luc tells the pastor. "What's your secret? Why the sudden change in the tone of these sermons?"

"This week, I'm drunk."

"Please don't say, 'drunk on the Holy Spirit,'" I tell him.

Brett looks a little defeated.

Luc says, "My wife thinks it's antidepressants."

"Your wife"—Brett glances at me but does not linger—"does not know everything."

Luc appears to find this incredibly funny. "Try telling her that."

"Do you have something to confess?" Brett is staring at my forehead as he says this, as if locking eyes produces too much intimacy and anything below that produces too much damnation.

"What exactly did you tell him?" I ask Duri, who suddenly is back to not being able to speak English again. He only blinks, shakes his head.

"I'm sorry, what are we talking about?" asks Luc. It's unclear who he is asking.

"Do you have the gift of prophecy, pastor?" I ask.

Brett considers this seriously. "Sometimes I can look out into the crowd and immediately tell who is trouble or in trouble. True story: Six months ago, a woman showed up to service wearing a crimson halter dress. I took one look at her from the stage and immediately thought to myself, now that's an adulteress—"

"How hot was this woman?" I cry, a little jealous.

"A week later, she shows up to my office seeking counsel. She's been fooling around on her husband and debating whether to tell him."

"Wait, you talking about my wife here? She has more than one red dress in her closet, I can tell you that," Luc interrupts.

Brett does not appear to get the joke, and if anything, finds our flippant approach to infidelity a bad sign that he hasn't been doing his job right. "I'm counseling the both of them now, but I can tell you this: I was right about her."

"Now is that a gift of prophecy or is she the only woman in the history of church to show up on Sunday in a red halter dress?" I would like to believe, but disbelief appears to be a condition I was born with.

"Whores, you can see them a mile away," Luc agrees. For this reason, we have stayed together despite all evidence directing us to the contrary.

Brett looks at Duri, then at us. I can tell that, having been plucked for ministry since a sophomore in college, he is not used to this level of skepticism.

"Well, good sermon," says Luc.

Duri bows, I give a little wave. Luc is right: we will never go back there again.

Back at the house, Duri is either restless or agitated or on something: he is back on his bed, trying his hand at another protracted nap, but from the kitchen table I can hear the springs in the mattress coiling then loosening like a hundred small metal teeth grinding against each other. At three o'clock, I turn on the television for tonight's pre–awards show and wait for him to emerge from his room, camera clicks and the soft murmur of reporters commentating being the modern-day equivalent of Sirens' calls. Duri emerges just before the first commercial break with his hair combed and a collared shirt underneath a blazer, resembling a Mormon kid on a job interview or maybe a dad on a date.

"You're so dressed up. Is there an afterparty you're going to or something?"

"You see The Band?" he asks instead.

"You would've heard the screaming if they'd shown up already." Based on yesterday's botched, silent ending to their musical performance on the comedy sketch show, who knows if this is still true. It seems empirically impossible that eighty-eight million fans could vanish overnight, or at least change their minds about the worthiness of their kings. What also seemed like an impossibility? That five hillbillies who had never even been to Seoul could turn themselves into the biggest hip-hop K-pop idols—previously an oxymoron in itself—and within a year, hurtle the tiny peninsula of a country from which they came into a global musical sensation whose songs, after breaking every other possible record (Billboard's, Grammy's, YouTube's, Guinness) started to break their own until worshipers from virtually every tribe and tongue started to learn Korean for no other purpose than to simply understand whatever lyrical sorcery came forth from their mouths. And even when Hangul proved to be harder than it looked, their devotees persisted in watching these boys, now men, live out their lives on screens in their mother tongue, not understanding a thing but still being unable to look away.

Ninety minutes in, after Duri's shirt collar has wilted and I've gotten up to retrieve snacks a half dozen times, Min's face is the first to peek out of the stretch limo. When his full form emerges, he looks like a walking, talking filter: each strand of his tufted hair has been individually assembled on top of his skull to resemble frosting, his skin lacquered. When Gwangju steps out behind him, a theme starts to emerge. His onyx suit has the same reflective sheen as Min's tin gray one, as if finely dusted with aluminum foil; his tresses have the identical congealed, packaged quality. Jae, Yoojin—they, too, bounce out of the vehicle in shiny three-piece ensembles and helmeted hair, one medieval, bronzed, and studded, making Jae resemble some made-over gladiator, the other brassy and layered with visible cuffs and shoulder pads, as if these could still protect a man.

"Heol," Duri mutters.

"What, do you not approve of what they're wearing?"

"Look at the face."

Duri is right. By some sleight of hand not yet widely known to makeup artists, the members' faces look flat, missing the usual lines and shadows that typically mark a human, like rings on an oak or scratches on a wrist. Their eyes, too, frequently altered to be various shades of water through colored lenses, are now all uniformly black, so dark it makes them appear a little dangerous, puddles a toddler could drown in. "Weird that they look like avatars of themselves."

"Fucking—" Then he says Pinocchio's real name.

Before I can ask or he can clarify, the screen shifts. The entertainment reporters and radio hosts and photographers are gone, having bloodlessly disappeared in response to some invisible finger snap, and the camera descends onto a black stage heavy with fog against a backdrop whose color reminds the audience of old jeans. Five anthropomorphic figures dot the gap where curtain meets floor, bodies contorted into various shapes modeled after Keith Haring subway art. The distant *ta-ta-ta-ta* on unseen drums gives way to what sounds like a hundred church ladies humming a hymnal bass reminiscent of breathing, although no actual choir emerges from stage left or right, not even from the goddamn ceiling. When the trill of Yoojin's characteristic falsetto interrupts the overture with its surgical perfection, the dancing commences: the figures, still in silhouette, start to dip, gyrating their narrow hips against the denim sky.

By the time they reach the first chorus, matching spotlights from above reveal the two center shadows to be Min and Gwangju just before they start to trade verses so fast it's impossible to tell whose lines belong to whom. At the refrain, another pair of lights from below unveil Jae to the left and, at last, Yoojin to the right. They've kept their hair but discarded their elaborate metallic jackets and waistcoats, donning instead molded onesies reminiscent of Marvel heroes.

"Have they been wearing these costumes underneath their suits this whole time?" I ask aloud.

Duri doesn't get the chance to speculate because now a fifth and

final set of lights from both above and below appears to illuminate
the last silhouette at the end of the formation. We see only his back
at first, but it's the familiar, exaggerated shape of a Dorito chip, all
shoulders and no ass, and when he raises his hand to heaven, long
index finger pointed at whatever celestial being resides on the other
side of the ozone, a sharp suction sound escapes Duri's mouth: the
finger on the screen is curved ever so slightly at the joint where prox-
imal meets middle phalanx.

I stare at him, and he glimpses down at his own matching hand,
and when we force our eyes back to the TV the figure has turned—
or rather, the podium he's been standing on has rotated, revealing
his true form: face saran-wrapped in the kind of glassy, shadowless
skin women like me whack off to, body in the same ridiculous luminescent suit to match his compadres, as if all things bright and
shiny could distract us from the harder questions of who the hell this
second Duri is, or perhaps more accurately what he is, and why, and
since when?

"Holy—"

"Ssi-bal," Duri finishes for me.

"Wait, are you—" I can't say it. It would make a fool of me. Sometimes unreliable narrators are made, not born.

Duri—if that is his name, if he is who he said—already has his
phone vertical against his cheek, but this time he is not translating for anyone, just biding his time for the requisite rings before the
beep, at which point he starts cursing the kind of universal expletives
you don't need Papago to understand. Ssi-bal, ssi-bal-saekki. I gather
that anything with ssi-bal in front of it means something hideous, but
it's unclear who he is talking to, himself or me or whoever is failing to
pick up on the other line or his alter ego belting out the second chorus line on the television screen, swaying its—his—hips in perfect
synchrony to the syncopated beat but whose skull remains utterly
locked, like Lot's wife fleeing Gomorrah if she had been a smarter

woman able to foresee the annihilatory consequences of turning her head. With dual spotlights shining on him from both the ceiling and floor, this face remains absolutely shadowless and eerily flat, as if deprived of its third dimension.

"Is that—"

"Ugh," says Duri.

"What?"

"Tsk, tsk." He pulls down on his own face, simulating the eventual effects of gravity on his currently perfect jowls, as if who we are is something we could take on and off. If only. "Shame on me."

"Are you apologizing for something?" An apology would be bad, very bad. It'd confirm everything I am thinking but not willing to say.

"I know this is going to happen. Now it is happening!"

"Tell me now or—" I don't mean it to be a threat. I consider where Luc is and what he is capable of; I think about the geolocations of my two children next to him and their capacities for long-term memory. Luc is taller than Duri, this is true. Also, thicker; with Americans there is almost never any competition, although it's not obvious in matters of physical force whether this is a benefit or liability. Before any ultimatums can be drafted or delivered, Duri jumps. Something on the screen dashes across my peripheral vision, and when I peek at where he is peering, I cannot believe it—

The security at awards shows, American ones at least, rival that of presidential visits and Swiss banks. It is tiered and assiduously layered, the closest thing these well-trained celebs get to cake. LA County Sheriff's Department, Beverly Hills PD, even the FBI—it is hard to underestimate the value of a human life when money, power, or fame is involved. The metal detectors at Le Cinq that Ilee, Kimme, and S had to go through the last time we could verify their whereabouts are child's play compared to what they've got going on outside the theater of tonight's ceremony where The Band is currently performing. We're talking unmanned aerial vehicles—souped-up versions of the drones Sam and Kilim briefly played with on Christmas morning before losing interest—two-way anonymous tip texting, at least a dozen people whose sole job is to monitor Twitter, modernity's equivalent of knocking on a million doors. There are the barricades to keep the peons and randos out and the months of background checks for every sound guy, caterer, and maid to weed out the ex-cons but let in anyone who's been growing a grudge as long as they have no priors. There are the contingency plans for all the disasters men can predict based on previous experience but none for the ones that have yet to happen. Any psychologist, or even your neighborhood psychic, will tell you that our ability to predict the future is strictly based on and constrained by what we've already seen. Good luck being prepared for something new.

And something new does happen.

It is happening right now against the protest of everything I think I know. It is not possible, it cannot be—

Center stage: an explosion. Before we even hear the boom, we already see audience members collapsing, chiffon gowns crumpling on the ground like deflating soufflés—flying objects ejected under certain conditions of enormous pressure move faster than sound, this we knew—then the screaming, it sounds like childbirth, involuntary and atavistic, interrupted finally by the actual bang, baritone, rumbling, before a ball of fire unfurls into white smoke, a beast in itself, while below everyone is out of their chairs, on the ground or running or clutching their useless lovers or phones or pearls, and by the time the uniformed men infiltrate the ballroom the smoke is gone, but so, too, is The Band. No one in the audience cares about the performers, but Duri and I, we are scanning the stage and there is nothing, just the remains of plywood shredded to resemble dirty tinsel and pockmarked holes, as irregular as a skin condition, on every possible surface, yet if we listen closely, above the rhythmic wailing of the humans on the floor, there is still the synth-y instrumental bridge of The Band's latest release, the song they were just performing, carrying on even in the absence of the voices to occupy them onstage—the show, apparently, does go on—and if we look closely in the putrefied air, opaque with residue, there's a flash here, a flicker really, a sliver of leg, there for a long millisecond, a patch of hand, still pointing with the curved finger to heaven—

"Is that what I think—"

"Hologram," Duri says, strangely calm given the sudden catastrophic turn of events. "You know augmented AI?"

"I've heard of augmented AI. 'Know' is a bit of a strong word."

Duri's face is almost kissing the television screen. He is squinting. "Where," he says, scanning the clumps of people.

"Are you looking for The Band?"

"There are no bodies onstage. They must be in audience. Or maybe backstage. The plan, I think, was a surprise. Ta-da, the performance is not really them, just avatars."

"You knew about this?" It is hard not to scream this.

Duri finally looks at me. "'Know is a strong word,'" he quotes. "Why do you think I am here?"

"I thought you were taking a mental health vacation." Admittedly, this sounds a little asinine coming out of my mouth now.

"Aish, contracts, woman, do you not know this? I have contract, I cannot just leave. Unless, of course, I have a replacement. Substitute."

The screen suddenly blackens into a prolonged moment of silence. Are we already mourning the dead? It doesn't take long for the broadcast to reappear, although now it is not the live telecast of the awards show. BREAKING NEWS scrolls across the top and bottom on the TV, as if we needed to read something twice to believe it. A reporter not dressed for work is already adjusting his mic. In the background we see lights and sirens blinking and blaring from stationary vehicles, occluding the historic theater venue and uneven trail of glitterati being escorted out but not allowed to leave.

The caption says, ACCIDENT AT MUSIC AWARDS SHOW. Who said it was accidental?

"Authorities have confirmed that there was an explosion onstage at the Dolby Theatre during tonight's Billboard Awards. We do not know the source or cause. It appears to have happened during the opening performance. Multiple injuries have been confirmed. The severity and identities of those affected remain unknown. You can see behind me that there are many, many ambulances. Multiple fire trucks. LAPD have been on the scene. I've just been informed that a counterterrorism unit is also en route. We are not saying this is a terrorist attack. We do not know what caused the explosion, if it was an accident. We just don't know," the reporter drones.

Duri is on the floor, prostrate, hand gripping the prickly hairs at the nape of his neck, as if surrendering to some impending brutality that awaits him.

At the risk of sending him over the cliff he is currently considering, I ask him anyway, "Wait, was the explosion part of the plan? I mean, a special effect or something?"

"No," he tells the hardwood floors. "I don't think. There is no way."

"You think it was an accident, then?"

He lifts his head. "We tour for seven years, never a single accident. One song, I stand on a horse on fire. Nothing bad happened. That"—he jabs a finger at the TV—"that is no accident."

"So, it was an attack." Me, empress of logic, especially when it's after the fact and too late for anything to be done.

When Duri shakes his head, the tip of his Anglo nose looks like it's nuzzling the ground. He doesn't say anything; he does not protest.

"I know you all have haters."

However true, it is the wrong thing to say. He releases his grip on the back of his head and his hands travel to his face, where they stay for a good long while until a little rivulet escapes the curve where thumb meets fingers.

"Are you crying?" I whisper. I have only seen grown men cry on two occasions—the first: my father, while watching an eighties-era miniseries about a supremely sexy orphan suffering from the same kind of parental neglect that he, too, liked to proffer; the second: my husband, when the unthinkable happened to his wife* and he both saw it coming and neglected to be around to stop it. If history is any indication, I didn't know what to do then either.

I scoot myself onto the ground and crawl over to the floorboards where Duri is, trying not to touch him and make things worse. I know the stereotypes birthed by K-Dramas (mostly written by women) claiming that Korean men cry all the time. It is their birthright and one of their most fuckable qualities, and yes, I'd seen the memes of The Band's members tearing up at various awards shows and surprise birthdays. Tears of joy are a different thing; there's something about happiness that changes the alchemy of salt water.

The reporter on the screen is blabbering, filling in the dead space between him and the camera with endless facts and figures, flexing his knowledge while proving his own uselessness in making sense of tragedy, which, if you think about, cannot be explained or made sense of because if it could, it wouldn't be so tragic. "We have confirmed reports that the explosion happened during the opening per-

---

*In one version of events, it's the world's most uncomfortable one-night stand between professor and student; in another, it's the kind of encounter #MeToo movements are founded upon. Across versions, it's dually forbidden for reasons related to status of both the marital and supervisorial kind. To make matters worse and in case it makes a difference to people, the professor in this case is a woman (also: Asian) and has been warned about this kind of thing for precisely those two reasons. The student is a man (also: white; not that it matters, of course), and younger to boot, with a GPA to consider. Together they raise all sorts of questions about consent (versus power) and whether women can be predators (or if the prey can do the penetrating) and most importantly (for our purposes here): Where the hell was her husband in all this?

The full details can be found in the novel to come.

formance by a popular K-pop group up for multiple awards tonight. The whereabouts of the performers are unknown. Their condition also unknown. At this point. No suspects have been apprehended."

"I love how this guy won't even come out and say 'The Band,' as if it's some big secret. Either he doesn't know or he's racist. Or maybe he doesn't know the name The Band because he is a racist. Also, talking about whereabouts and suspects like these guys are the ones behind it? Racist again!" Now I'm blabbering, too, but I can't seem to help myself. "When was the last time a K-pop group was nominated for this many Billboard awards? It's not like there are so many K-pop groups on the Billboard charts and he can't remember which one."

Duri pops up his head, cheeks damp and eyelids like newly leavened dough. I want to lick those tears straight off. I don't.

"Girl band," he says.

"There's more than one girl band. Which one are you talking about?"

"Before us, three girls. Korean. They sing, they rap, they dance. Came to America and had a hit single, somewhere on Billboard, not number one or two but not number ninety-nine either."

"I vaguely remember this from like a decade ago," I admit. "I had a friend, Andrew, who was into them. Put their album cover as his profile pic on Facebook, Twitter, everything. What was their name again?"

Duri only shakes his head, refusing to say it out loud but allowing himself to list the members instead. "Kimme, Ilee, S."

"You know them?"

Both of Duri's eyebrows arch as his mouth stretches into a grimace like a man forced to play messenger and bracing himself to be shot. "S is not alive."

"Oh. I'm sorry, I had no—"

"You don't know the story?"

"I didn't even know who you were when we first met until you called yourself Pretty Boy and it jogged my memory of something I saw online. I live under a rock."

Duri sighs, standing slowly, as if moving through water. He grabs his phone. "I tell you the whole thing," he says, glancing wearily at the television screen still stuck on the same scene of ambulances and patrol lights and not a single person who knows what's what. Sitting back down on the couch, he taps the little parrot on his device and brings it to his lips.

"Kimme, Ilee, and S were our producer's first idol group. The original version of us. They were supposed to be The Band, except the girls protested that they didn't like the name, thought it sounded too generic, or maybe just too masculine, and so right before debuting, they changed it. Their first single was even more popular than ours. It hit number one in Korea within days. America was the next target; it always is. They came to LA first—not far from your house—and got introduced to this former idol who was the first Korean musician to break into the U.S. market." He mumbles a name I don't care to remember. "If you were Korean, you would know him. He took them out to this club called Le Cinq on their first night in America and—"

At this, Duri stops. I wonder if he expects me to guess what happens next.

"You can't stop now," I tell him.

"He"—the grimace on his face is back—"Ssi-bal."

"I've seen some shit. You can say it."

"There is a video. Ilee recorded it on her phone. Then she shared it because we cannot see the future."

"God, do not make me guess. I don't want to go down a list of progressively worse things one man could do to a woman."

"He is married, you have to remember. In Korea, we do not even kiss in public. In this club, this idol, he—" Duri pauses again. "I will find the video. We do not scrub things from the internet as well as you Americans do. I am sure it is still posted some—ah, here."

He hands me his phone. The recording is already playing, its resolution grainy and unfiltered, but it does not take any squinting to see a girl in a bandage dress pressed against the erotic red vinyl of a booth, a man pressing his face against her dim neck occluded by shadows. Techno disco-pop is humming in the background, but a sharp "hajimaaa" escapes from her mouth, to which the gentleman—he is dressed as such, cuffs, collar, skinny tie, the works—replies by scolding her name. "S, S, S," he hisses, impersonating a snake or maybe just the devil himself. Both of her hands press against his breastplate like she is trying to push open—or away—a heavy door, but either she is too weak or he is too determined because he doesn't move, does not budge in the slightest. If anything, he looks a little amused. His own hand, so pale it glows in the dark, worms itself between her knees and scoots upward—

I hand the phone back to Duri. "I get the point." I don't need to see what happens next.

"Afterward, things get a little blurry," he tells me. "No one knows exactly the order of events and our producer never talks about it, but we all read the news. Ilee and S use the video to blackmail this man for money, threaten to turn it over to Dispatch or post it on YouTube if he does not pay—"

"He's that rich?"

"I heard he had two cars that suggested he was."

"I thought they already had a hit single. What did they need the money for?"

"Trainee debt. All those years living in the dormitories, the voice lessons, dance lessons, meals, personal trainers. Once they did debut, the promotional advertising, flights, per diems. They have to pay producers and songwriters and studios too. It takes the average idol group at least two years to pay it back, and by then many of them are already done."

"You knew this and joined The Band anyway?"

"Our producer got rid of trainee debt after what happened with S."

"Her blackmailing plan didn't work?"

"The idol, he turned the video over to the police in Korea and reported them for blackmailing him. S and Ilee were arrested, brought up on charges."

"They punished the women* instead? You're fucking kidding me."

"I am not a funny guy," Duri retorts.

"I'm sorry, is it just me or does she look—in the video—non . . . I mean, she doesn't appear to really, you know—"

He raises both hands, either in surrender or protest, as if innocence could be achieved simply by not getting involved.

"Consent" is the hardest word in the English language, so hard I don't even know if it translates properly. I say instead, "She doesn't exactly look willing is what I'm trying to get at."

Duri blinks. At fan meets in Seoul and Busan (or Incheon or Daegu), girls—they were always girls—would routinely bring all kinds of costume accessories for The Band to dress up in during these photo ops as they wrung their hands and squealed and hyperventilated and professed their love even as they treated the boys with a level of objectification normally reserved for porno stars and sex dolls—objects not typically known for being well-loved. Furry ears, hats, bows, headbands, tiaras, oversized barrettes in the shape of small fruits or similarly sized rodents proved to be the most popular, but on several occasions, somebody handed over a goddamned

---

*Upon further reflection, I should not have been surprised. See: Paula Broadwell—Petraeus's biographer, mentee, and once-lover who lost her job, her reputation, and all future professional prospects for the sole crime of sleeping with a five-star general (while he traded his CIA post for a better paid gig at a New York private equity firm, a nominal affiliation with Harvard, and a standing advisory role at the White House); or how about Monica Lewinsky—the twenty-two-year-old intern who fell for her boss and then spent the next two decades paying for it until her TED talk on cyberbullying finally turned her prospects around, while said boss remained in office as the leader of the free world, published a few books, campaigned for other Democrats, and came this close to becoming First Husband.

wedding veil. The members have gamely dressed up as bunnies, gi-
raffes, various Disney characters, fantastic beasts. Duri once got an
egregious powder-blue baby bonnet that he had no choice but to
tie around his head. He held his smile and crossed his thumb and
forefinger into a characteristic heart, waited for the moment to pass.
That was just the start of it. Other fans asked to touch his face, which
he allowed, and they did with impunity, performing the kind of intimate kneading and stroking he expected from a shu gua session or
deep tissue massage. Still others have asked him to serenade them,
dance for them (what's the difference between that and what strip-
pers do, I want to know), propose marriage, and draw a ring on their
finger. A person can do anything when the unit of time is in minutes.
In his mind, willingness was beside the point. Willingness was never
a question anyone asked, and if they did, it was with the understanding that a good person would always oblige.

He did, and they were happy, and after seven years of this, seven
years of endless worshipful attention paired with equally endless
obligatory moments, seven years of reprieve from women never having to say no—they never say no anymore—he doesn't know if he is
even qualified to answer the question.

History hinges or breaks on the things we do not do.

"They go to jail for this?" I ask when it becomes clear that no justice will be served, so measuring blame is all there is left to do.

"S, she died."

"In jail?" I couldn't believe it.

"At home," he corrects.

"She was sick or something?" I already know this is not true, but
it seems wrong to malign the dead by instantly assuming something
worse.

Duri spells out the accoutrements used to achieve a more instan-
taneous ending. "Bathtub. Shower rod. A belt."

"My God," I say.

"I doubt God wants part of this," he answers. (On this, Duri is wrong; the problem of suffering appears to be a problem for everyone except the Almighty himself.)*

"Did she leave a note?" I want to know.

Duri raises both brows, creating a soft pleat in an otherwise glassy forehead. "Half the population thought she was a slut. The other half thought she was both a slut and a blackmailer. What is there to say to a world like that?"

"And the others?"

"Ilee posted the video online, then disappeared. She was supposed to be on house arrest before sentencing. Fugitive, is that what you call her? Now, maybe she is in North Korea or Switzerland or Los Angeles. Kimme, left by herself, tried a solo act. It did not work. The former idol—he is still alive, I am sure. Guys like him never die, or do not die soon enough. What else is there?"

"Your producer, Pinocchio—"

"He only works with boys now."

"That's a little drastic. It sounds like punishing the victim—"

"If you cannot save them, the least you can do is not lead them where you know there are wolves. No?"

"I'm sorry," I tell him, because there is nothing else to say.

"The person I am most sorry about is Ilee, do you not agree? She is still paying for this."

"Frankly, I'm surprised she hasn't turned up all these years. If they

---

*The uninspired always ask why a decent God could put up with horrible things happening to good people, but turns out, the most godforsaken people in the world are also the ones who believe in him the most (for the empirically minded, see: Gray and Wegner 2010). When incomprehensible things happen and there isn't a clear worthy person to blame, God—who apparently can do anything yet remains above the fray of human feelings—always gets all the credit. You may not like him, but you necessarily have to believe he exists. For an incorporeal, invisible deity whose primary agenda is to inspire belief among mortals, that may not be a bad trade. After all, isn't the opposite of love not hate but indifference?

can find old Nazis hiding in Argentina, I'm surprised they can't find a girl rapper wanted for blackmail."

"I doubt they are looking very hard. It would not be difficult for her to live in a big country like this where no one knows her, waiting."

"Waiting for what?"

"Until she can make a new name for herself, be known for something other than the failed K-pop group that preceded The Band."

"I wonder where she is now?"

Duri looks at the screen, now shifted to a press conference with an older white gentleman behind a podium, decked out in cornflower blue and a multitude of patches and pins, flanked by a gaggle of still older white dudes in various shades of sky. They all look related. But then again, justice, law, power—these are but branches on the same patriarch, a singular family tree. "Maybe she is watching," he suggests.

Pastor Brett was not the only person with the gift of prophecy.

16

Spiritual Gifts

The good news is that they are only numbering the injured, much to everyone's shock and awe but especially to the sheriff in Vermeer's favorite color, who looks a little disappointed that there are no dead bodies to account for. Thirteen have been transported to Cedars-Sinai, three in critical care. A true miracle, all the newscasters and analysts and doctors with podcasts are saying. Unbelievable, Twitter echoes. If this had been a semiautomatic rifle instead of a bomb, the experts used to commentating on this sort of pain surmise, it'd be a different story. If there had been performers actually on the stage in the flesh instead of CGI, we'd all be holding candlelight vigils.

It seems inappropriate, morbid even, to prematurely mourn those stuck in operating rooms when the status of life and limb is still being determined. No one does. Instead, we all just watch the TV. It is much more interesting than whatever sadness is whirling around in our own lives.

Duri has his phone on speaker and is dialing, dialing, dialing between sips of straight Bacardi he found in the back of the fridge,

Coke be damned. Each time, the dial tone drones on ceaselessly until a beep or his own thumb ends the petitioning. It appears that no one cares that he, lost for so many days, now is trying to get himself found. On the fifth call, a distant male voice answers. "Yeo-bo-se-yo?" The sound is small and far away.

"Aigoo, did you forget my number already?" Duri slurs in his native tongue. My phone's Google Translate AI is apparently well trained in parsing the speech of drunks.

"Sang Du-ri?"

"It is me. Or my kidnapper, I suppose. Do I sound like a kidnapper to you?"

"Now is not the time for joking."

"Now is precisely the time for joking because what else can we do at a time like this? Nothing, nothing. Are you there with The Band, Pino—"

"No, young idiot, I am in Seoul where I always am. At headquarters, in my office. You have been gone for ten days and you already forget how we operate?"

"How sweet, you are counting the days since my disappearance. I always knew you loved me."

"Enough. Are you watching this abomination on the television?"

"Why do you think I am calling?"

"I cannot get a hold of any of them. Not even Min is picking up, and he has never failed to answer the phone when I call."

"What about the staff? Manager, bodyguard, the goddamn hairstylist?"

"I managed to get through to one or two, but it was gibberish. Everyone is separated and police are detaining people and half of them do not even speak English all that well. This is the worst thing that can ever happen—"

"Worse than what happened with the girls?"

"Excuse me?"

"Kimme, S, Ilee." Their names need no translation, so I finally glance away from my phone to find Luc and the kids shuffling noiselessly up the stairs in their matching crew socks. My husband is looking at me with his lower jaw jutting from the rest of his bearded face, a judgmental look I know well and therefore am also well-practiced at ignoring.

"Aish, are you seriously bringing that up right now?" Pinocchio cries, loud enough for me to once again forget the more mum members of my family.

"Tragedy begets tragedy," Duri replies, strangely philosophical for an aspiring alcoholic.

"You know, I did get a warning. This note . . . Hold on—"

Duri looks up at me. "This guy," he says in English, shaking his head. He hands me his glass emptied of its contents and juts his chin toward the kitchen. It's unclear whether he is signaling for me to leave or demanding more Bacardi. It's also unclear which message is more offensive. Apparently I lack the self-respect to say no to men I've seen—or imagined—naked because the next thing you know, I'm in front of the fridge when Pinocchio's voice emanates from the other room.

"This note, it says, 'I am coming for your second baby.' What do you think?"

"'Second baby' makes it sound like the kind of note your first baby would write."

"I tried to make many groups before The Band—"

"But only one debuted. The girl group—"

"They disbanded so long ago."

"The Beatles disbanded. H.O.T. disbanded. Wonder Girls, Miss A. When one member hangs herself and another disappears after they both get charged with blackmail—"

"Before you say something more that you have to apologize to me for later, remember this: The Band only exists because I could not save those girls and had to start over."

"All the more reason your firstborn is after your second born. I assume you do not get notes like this every day."

"I never get fan mail or hate mail. I am not famous enough."

"This was mailed to your office?"

"I found it under my door, but it could have been mailed or dropped off. Who knows? My secretary is such a babo.* She is not the brightest or most organized—"

"Why else do you keep her around?"

"Have you seen her recently? Her eyes, they did such a good job."

"If you hired her for that, who is the babo now?"

"You know, you should not be talking, considering you are the one in hiding with no end game in sight."

"You have not asked me where I am."

"I figured that you would not answer if I did. If you wanted me to know where you are, you would have told me."

"I always forget how smart you are."

"No, I should have passed this damn note to the National Intelligence Service or the FBI or at least security. We were warned, and all I did was pass it to the members, who did not take it seriously either."

"Wait, you think the note is referring to the bomb?"

"You five are my only babies. Who else?"

"Maybe you should start considering, as the Americans say"— Duri suddenly switches to English, which I take as permission to come back to the living room—"'diversifying your portfolio.'"

"I cannot believe you are still joking at such a time as this."

"I am not joking; I am giving you a hint."

"You are with an American right now, is that what you are implying?"

Duri glances in my direction as I hand him another glass filled

---

*Google Translate knows everything except how to swear in Korean, apparently.

with clear liquid. I don't tell him it's only half Bacardi (the other half: water). "Sort of," he admits.

"This is some friend of yours?"

"You can call her that."

"It is a woman?" Pinocchio is verifiably yelling.

"Would you rather I be with a man?"

A documented first: our impresario appears not to know what to say.

Duri says, "She is also married."

"You are killing me."

"But do not worry, she is not married to me."

"Am I supposed to be relieved?"

"Noona too—" He looks at me, whispering, "How old are you?"

"Really?" I answer.

Duri says instead into the phone, "Also with kids. Two! Honhyeol. And so very cute, like me."

"I did not say anything about your little music video that started this need of yours to flee, but I am starting to get the impression that the solution is worse than the problem."

"You have the holograms already from all those full-body scans we did for the last album, and reference photos, it looks like. On top of the album, we recorded all my voice samples for future songs. Other than missing me from interviews, in some sense, I never left."

"Did you see the beginning of the performance, before the bomb? We debated whether to have just you as CGI or the whole band and decided it would be less suspicious if all five of you were computer-generated."

"It fooled my friend here." Duri shoots me another pointed glance, but I'm too embarrassed to apologize. "For a long minute, she suddenly thought I was an imposter impersonating the real Sang Du-ri. If it were not for the bombing, she might have thrown me out of her house."

"I didn't actually threaten you—" I protest, but it's useless speaking when not spoken to—at least when men are around, I've noticed. He swats in my general direction.

"As much as I would like to spare you from the equation entirely and make Sang Du-ri into the next Hatsune Miku or turn The Band into the Korean Gorillaz, I do want to know if you plan on coming back. Is this you handing me back the keys to the kingdom?"

"Hatsune Miku only has 2.5 million Facebook fans. Do you mean to insult me?"

"Correction: Hatsune Miku is not real and still has 2.5 million fans. Hatsune Miku has no search results on Dispatch. Or TMZ, just ask your little friend over there in America. Also: Hatsune Miku does not crack and is less of a liability than you."

"I am not cracking."

"You are never going to compete with a sixteen-year-old ageless robot with blue pigtails for infallibility."

Duri winces a little when he considers this. "And the fans?"

"In interviews, premieres, what do you always say about them?"

"It is all for the fans. Everything we do is for them."

"Exactly. Think about it. Fans will be able to upload their own fan art, make you look however they want. You will never have to wear lip gloss or bleach your hair pink again. They can write the songs they want you to sing them, even collaborate and add their own instrumentation. You will not need to send every song lyric you write up the chain to feminists and historians and linguists and urban dictionaries to make sure you are not saying something offensive that will get you canceled again or that sounds like a racial slur in a different language. It is the future. More than that, it is the natural conclusion to where the fandom is going, where it wants to end up. Total control over the artist, absolute power."

"I like wearing lip gloss. It feels nice—"

"Are you wearing it right now?"

"Right now, I cannot, I am drinking my—" Duri turns to me, mouths, "How many is this?"

Before I can count for him the number of empty mason jars congregated on the floor between us, he asks the producer, "Do you miss me?" His voice is small all of a sudden.

Pinocchio's pause lasts a beat too long. Duri says instead, "I do not miss you that much. But I miss them."

On cue, as if words were gods that could speak worlds into existence, The Band appears on the television screen before us, their heads turned downward as they walk toward the blazed camera lights outside, bodies and limbs intact, hair and makeup too, surrounded by familiar but less-famous faces, an exodus of the monied and inflamed.

Duri's phone slips out of his hand, and he doesn't bother to watch it conjoin with the travertine tiles or see its screen turn black as Pinocchio's line drops. A headless voice emanates from the television:

"As you can see, officials are guiding the safe exit of remaining uninjured attendees of tonight's tragic music awards show from the venue. Our sources have confirmed that all persons will be questioned. FBI agents are completing their sweep of the grounds for evidence and possible other devices."

"They're alive," I say.

"Holy, holy." Duri sounds like a Justin Bieber song.

"You believe in God now?"

He declines to look at me. "I go to church with you, I talk to pastor."

"You asked him if he was taking antidepressants. That's not exactly a great display of faith."

"No, I told him I was living with a married woman. You know, confession?"

"You did not." A pause. "We're not Catholic!" Then it dawns on me. "Is that why Pastor Brett asked me if I had anything to confess?"

Duri shrugs. "I am not the one with a husband."

"Luc does not—" "Care" is the wrong word. I suspect my husband loves me in ways I can never quite understand and so I'm always left questioning his motives. His tolerance for my sins—peccadilloes they are not—is, as Jesus said about his own tortured relationship with his beloved, both the cornerstone and a stumbling block of our marriage. He lets me do what (and who) I want. But does that make him the world's most forgiving husband or its most indifferent lover?*

Duri offers nothing, only stares at me with an expression I haven't seen before. It's both tender and foreign, so much so that I'm forced to look away.

"I have kids I have to put to bed," I tell him, suddenly remembering the pair of small humans whose existence is an answer to the unspoken question posed here.**

Upstairs, Sam passes me flossing in the bathroom with a new set of burrows between his brows. "How long is this guy staying?" he says, sectioning off his own strand of waxed string. It sounds less like a question and more of a complaint.

"You don't listen to The Band?" I ask instead. What do they call this—the Socratic method?

He shrugs. "I see people dancing to their songs on TikTok," he concedes. Apparently two can play this game of not answering the other person's questions. Then, a concession: "I'm not a teenage girl," he says.

---

*Also possible: that kink and love are not neighbors in the least but vast islands of their own making, self-sustaining and so wrapped up in their own ecosystems that they can't help but neglect each other's existence, such that having one should not (theoretically) threaten having another. But then again, some things are impossible to prove and even harder to live by.

**You thought it; I'll say it: Why are we together?

"Neither am I," I remind him.

"What are you doing, then?" Another statement parading as a question but sounding like anything but.

"How old are you again?"

"Ten."

"It was a joke. I obviously know how old my own child is."

"When's my birthday?"

"I think you're confusing me with your father. He's the only one in this house who can't remember when his firstborn showed up."

"Kilim doesn't know either. Obviously."

"Kilim knows your birthday is three days after his, so technically he's ahead of Dad on that one."

"Are you two getting a divorce?" Sam asks, no warning whatsoever. It's his favorite question.

The floss dribbles out of his mouth. My jaw, too, has left the building. "Whatever gave you that idea?" Every time, I still manage to be surprised.

"Is Duri my new daddy?"

"Ha, I wish!" This is the funniest thing I've heard all day. "Also, you should stop asking if every dude who comes over to this house is your stepdad-in-training. I don't know who gave you this complex."

"It's either you or Dad."

"Has anyone ever told you that you should try acting your age?"

"Has anyone ever told their child that being mature is a bad thing?"

"I give up," I tell him. "You win. But there are no new-dad prizes involved in any of the games we are playing."

"There are other prizes?"

I grin. "Maybe not for you."

Sam rolls his eyes and adjusts the headphones he wears continuously around his neck like a collar, the prepubescent-boy version of a blankie or maybe the adult-male version of a pacifier. "Gross, Mom," he tells me, already walking away.

When it is Luc's turn to stalk by the bathroom to check upon my whereabouts, a similar pair of valleys have formed in the undulating grooves between his eyebrows. "You hear about The Band?" he says.

"You mean the explosion?"

"Your boy downstairs is doing okay?"

"He's watching the news still, so no, probably not."

"You think hiding up here in the bathroom flossing away is a nice thing to be doing right now?"

"I figured you'd want help putting the kids to bed."

"First time for everything."

"Now you're not even being fair."

"Kilim is already asleep on our bed. Knocked himself out watching shark videos on Instagram while waiting for his mother to come upstairs. You know it's nine o'clock."

"It was eight thirty when I walked up the stairs, so either you or my phone is lying."

"Do what you want."

"I don't want anything. I'm just trying to make sure everyone is in bed."

"I'm going to bed myself," Luc declares. "But you should probably go downstairs and make sure your boy doesn't have a panic attack."

"Please stop referring to him as that."

Luc raises his shoulders. A decade in this institution called marriage, it's hard to care about semantics and the logistical details. "They just caught the guy, it sounds like."

"Wait, what?"

"Girl," he corrects.

But I am already trailing down the stairs.

17

The Lost & Found

Duri is not there. The living room looks abandoned, mason jars strewn about like wayward toys, his phone still lying face up in the shadows of the couch. On the TV screen is a girl—a woman, really—handcuffed and expressionless, flanked as she walks into the glaring Angeleno evening.

I can't believe it, but it's true: she's Asian.

In her black-and-white catering outfit, her ethnicity is technically the last thing I notice. The starched shirt, lopsided from either wear or being manhandled by a bevy of FBI agents eager to make a point; the ill-fitting vest, unflattering from the start; the stupid teal bow tie—it's all an abomination to the senses. Only when she looks directly into the camera do her eyes give away her ancestry. They are shaped like tears, freakishly large and mammalian and threatening to overwhelm the rest of her small, unadorned face.

SUSPECT IN CUSTODY, says the scrolling red ribbon decorating the bottom of the TV screen.

"The full identity of the woman shown here has not been

confirmed by investigators, but sources suggest that she is a former K-pop idol," the anthropomorphic TV voice drones.

By the time the reporter comes back on, he is somber with discovery. "Now, keep in mind, this is not the same K-pop idol group that was performing tonight onstage and up for multiple awards," Captain Obvious tells America just in case they, in their ethnocentrism, had presumed that the quota for K-pop groups in America is a strict n = 1. "The detainee was apparently part of a three-man—correction, three-woman—group in the early aughts named—"

"Duri," I call out, waiting for a miracle. He is not in the kitchen, his room, or either downstairs bathroom. The garage is well-stocked with sedans but devoid of people, dead or alive. His Land Rover is no longer kissing the curb, a bad sign for everyone involved.

I've got a bad habit of looking for things in places I know they can't be found (spent money in wallets, deleted emails in inboxes, high school boyfriends on Instagram, the meaning of life in the dual heads of men), so in a bout of magical thinking, I dart back up the stairs to look for Duri in bedrooms and showers, those sacred spots where our most obscene moments like to happen. I never said I was a hero; I'm most useless in moments like this.

Sam's room, dimly shrouded in the soft blue glow of a luminescent screen, titters with the distant banter of white boys on TikTok whose twangy, coastal accents make them sound both a little dumb and super rich, an apparently irresistible (aspirational?) combination. Next door, Kilim's bedroom is brightly lit but as devoid of him as it is replete with the debris of his presence: trains divorced from their tracks, amputated LEGO figurines, battery-drained planes.

Across the hall in our room, Luc is spread across the bed like a winged bird. When I jab his shoulder, he lifts his head up with such violence he appears to sprain his own neck.

"Fucking A." He squints. "What now?"

"I was looking for Duri," I tell him. "Although now I'm also wondering where our other child is."

"Mother of the Year," he announces before lifting the duvet to reveal a catatonic Kilim tucked below his armpit, asleep but still gripping a phone paused in the middle of a shark video.

"Really?" I demand. "And here I thought I was merely going for Wife of the Year."

When Luc bursts out laughing just as his face lands back into the pillow, it makes a wet, smothered gurgle, like a man caught in the throes of autoasphyxiation. "You might be the least domestic person—"

"I cook all our meals! I clean the house—"

"Yes, but how much of that is for us versus you trying to prove a point?"

"I don't see the difference, as long as it gets done. Also, what exactly am I proving?"

"You understand glory, achievement, all that stuff you were raised on that you can outdo everyone else on, man, woman, or child, because being the best at something is its own drug and that's why you never so much as touched a joint or got a hangover. You also understand sex, of walking into a room and immediately asking yourself who you want, and more importantly, who wants or maybe just needs you, because for an insecure person there's no greater aphrodisiac in the world than being sought after—"

"You're making me sound like the devil with a savior complex."

Luc shakes his head. "You've got bigger problems than that. You don't understand how to be both bored and happy."

I look at my husband. "Are you both bored and happy with me?"

He sits up because no good thinking ever happened to a man lying down. "I was, until you took boredom to be a marital disease we had to cure, then the solution turned out to be worse than the problem."

"If you're talking about Loyle, your friend who nearly broke our marriage, that was a misunderstanding, a bad game of telephone where I took your fantasies about having something to fight for—having to compete for me, I mean—a little too literally, and you, you failed to adequately explain to me the difference between a cuckold and a cheat. If you're talking about who came after, when you were gone, busy rethinking your life choices, that—I wasn't exactly a willing participant. You know this as well as me."

"I think you're forgetting about Duri," Luc says, suddenly a little sad. "Is he not the latest cure for whatever unhappiness you think you've got?"

Sometimes the truth is a little bird that comes and softly sits on your shoulder, whispering to you when you are least looking for it. Other times it is a bag of bricks delivered without warning on your head and you want nothing more than to die from the knowledge. "And all this time I thought I was the one trying to save him."

"Good luck with that."

"You don't understand, the chick—that woman they caught—he knows her, she was the original—"

"I don't think you heard me the first time. I said, good luck—"

"Do you not understand the gravity of this situation?"

"What do you think your boy's going to do, drive off a cliff?"

"We do live on a mountain. They don't call it the Hill for nothing. He wouldn't have to drive far."

"No one calls it the Hill. You're confusing us with Laguna Beach and that show, *The Hills*."

"Are you really correcting my geography right now?"

"What would you like for me to be doing?"

"Help me look for him."

"And our dear children? If we wake them up and drag them along on a midnight excursion so Mommy can look for her new boyfriend, they will be in therapy for the rest of their lives."

"He's not my boyfriend. You know this."

"We're at that point in our marriage where I don't know anything, but I do know this: that boy dies on your watch, you're going to have some explaining to do. How many fans do they have again?"

"You *do* think he's going to drive off a cliff!"

"Like I said, I don't know anything."

"Lord."

"Now you start crying out to Jesus."

"Jesus take the wheel?" A bad joke even in the best of times.

Luc roots around the bedside table for his car keys, tosses them.

"Take the Volvo," he says, an olive branch. "You'll have a better chance of survival, maybe."

"What do you think I'm going to do, crash myself?" I demand, already at the top of the stairs.

"Two emotional Asians driving around a low mountain range at night," he mutters. "I will be indebted to God forever if I see the both of you at breakfast in the morning."

Palos Verdes at night is exactly like Palos Verdes in the morning: empty and gorgeous and so boring that sometimes you forget to breathe. To preserve the view of the evening sky, streetlights are as rare as domestic cars. Driving from the campy pastoral courtyards of Malaga Cove to the winding equestrian lanes of Rolling Hills Estates, I do not see a single Ford or Chevy and require only one hand to count the number of lampposts. Here, even the old white people who voted for Trump don't drive American, *America First* be damned.

I pass the curved gully overgrown with grass and weedy chaparral where Tiger Woods—another Asian—had his latest car accident— sans toxicology report—and I try to count the number of Bacardis I poured for Duri before heading upstairs and leaving him to his own bad ideas. I am very, very bad at predicting the future or foreseeing the consequences of my own actions, it turns out. When he is trying to be kind, Luc calls me oblivious. When the time for kindness has passed, he uses more truthful words, like "autistic." (He means on the spectrum.) I have never been tested because I am curious about everything except the true causes of my own behavior, about which I am rather fatalistic. Also: I have no interest in finding out about the status of things for which there are no cures.

By the time I reach PCH, the choices are to turn right for the proletarian docks of San Pedro, where my favorite history teacher still lives with his forgiving wife, or left, for the progressively more highfalutin beaches of Redondo, Hermosa, then Manhattan, the most highfalutin of them all. I pick left; I can't remember the last time I saw an Asian person other than myself in San Pedro, and even then, I wasn't supposed to be there. When PCH forks, I am not paying attention, I am looking for an international pop star, so I veer left instead of right and do not know what street I am on anymore because I never drive anywhere. The year before I met Luc, I totaled three Volvos in a row, so as far as I could tell, the whole point of getting hitched was to conjoin with someone who is a better driver than me and thereby preclude my own statistically likely automotive death. The veiny little lanes of the Riviera Village deposit me back onto Esplanade, where I pass all the reverse alphabetized side streets—I, H, G, F, E—and behold! A miracle.

Double-parked in a red strip of the fire lane is a black Land Rover, car lights still on but otherwise emptied of life. The little barcodes guarding the windshield and back windows give away that it's a rental.

I park on the other side of the street where the meters are. There is no way Duri drove his car all the way here to take a nap in the back seat, so there is no point checking. A concrete ramp descends onto the sidewalk where sand meets pedestrian lane. There are no joggers or bikers or cheap dates at this hour, not even an errant homeless person—LA, lacking the more strident liberalism of certain other

Californian counties, believes in social justice in theory but property values in practice.

Twenty yards in, there is a white shirt glowing in the dark. The black hair above it and black pants below it disappear seamlessly into the night sky, making the figure seem like an apparition, or maybe just wayward laundry.

The sand, it's soft and cold and its constant give makes it no fun to walk over; it's no thrill to trample over something that's always accommodating the shape of your foot. Perhaps that is why after a string of negotiated—let's call them "indiscretions," of which the history teacher was the latest and the last, I had given up on the idea that enough wrongs could make a right. The problem with sin is less that it's wrong and more that it demands to be repeated. Because how else can you live with yourself? Then Duri came along. We plan, God giggles; there are few more reliable laws of the universe.

Duri, Duri. The wind has scrambled his hair across his face, but that fox's chin and Edenic mouth, a woman can recognize anytime, anywhere.

"Is this still heaven?" I ask him, sitting down.

When he doesn't answer, I barge on. "You said right after you debuted, you came here once and told Gwangju this must be what heaven—"

"I remember."

"And now?"

"You know problem with heaven?" he asks.

"Tell me," I say.

"Once you see heaven," he says, "everything else looks like hell."

I look at him, and it's tempting to think you can talk a person out of whatever the monsters are in his head. As if monsters were rational beings who obey the laws of Aristotelian logic and linear thinking, rather than fantastic beasts of our own creation who know no rules but their own.

What's also tempting to believe: that the depressed or anxious or unwell person hates themselves, that their mama didn't hug them enough or their father loved money or pussy or drank too much (the top three offenders as far as fathers go), or some other tragedy—institutional, interpersonal, or divine—befell them and rendered them neurochemically incapable of appreciating their own worth. In reality, I suspect such a person loves themself just fine, loves themself as much as I love me. If they didn't, they wouldn't be here, because they remain the only person they would die for at a moment's notice. What is really going on is that they are trapped inside a burning building* for which there are no marked exits, a burning building they lovingly attend to and maybe sometimes even stoke, not because they are self-enabling, but because they have no other place to call home, at least not now, at least not yet. We, on the outside, don't know much either—we have our hoses and ladders and trucks, and if we are lucky, and if we hear the alarm and get there in time, and if the wind isn't too bad, then sometimes we get to call ourselves heroes and feel good about the initials after our names.** Other times—other times we do not.

"You wanted out?" I ask. "Short of sui—" The word catches in my throat. I can't say it. "—permanent solutions for temporary problems, fleeing the motherland and shacking up with a stranger seemed like the compassionate thing to do for all parties involved—The Band, the producer, the fandom?"

"Why you ask questions when you already know the answer?" Duri replies.

"Why did you come here if it no longer looks like heaven?"

He points to the water foaming inches away from his toes, which

---

*See also: Wallace 2011.
**P, h, and D.

are long and reedy like the rest of him. "I walk far enough in, soon the real heaven comes to me."

"Drowning is the worst way to die," I tell him.

"You know this?"

"I don't have to stick my finger in a pencil sharpener to know it's a bad idea."

"You never want to die?"

"I do. Not infrequently. Less often than when I was young. Say what you will about marriage or kids, but they do help when it comes to that. Give you ties to hold on to when you don't feel like playing any longer. I want to die, but I want to live more."

"Your husband, he loves you?"

After what Luc said earlier, this is the second-funniest thing I've heard all day. "You have no idea."

"That means yes, or no?"

"My husband loves me so much that he would rather me be with anyone else if it'll make me happy for a little while. But he has never left. Not for long anyway. I wrote a whole book about it. When I head home after this, I'll send you a copy, something to remember me by."

"I am leaving? I need to remember you?"

"If it makes you feel any better, you're welcome to forget."

"Some things are impossible," he says, a little sad.

"You didn't ask me if I love my husband," I observe.

"I know already."

"It's that obvious?" And I thought I was being so careful.

"If you did not love him, you would be with me already."

I do not like surprises, but some surprises are preferable to others. "I didn't think I stood a chance."

Now it is Duri's turn to laugh. "You probably do not," he agreed. "You would have tried harder, though."

"I don't like to beg."

"Is that what you call it?"

"You know," I tell him, "your English is pretty good. You don't even need that silly translation app."

"Do not tell anyone. Otherwise, they will make me talk when right now all we have to do is sit still and smile while Min answers the questions."

"I knew it!" I cried. "You looked way too comfortable talking to Pastor Brett earlier. And I figured you wouldn't show up here alone with no entourage if you couldn't hold your own." Then it strikes me: "Why'd you bother with using the stupid parrot at all, then?"

Duri shrugs. "I wanted to see if you would still talk to me when it was difficult and required extra effort."

"You know, short of the devil himself, I don't know any person who tries to test me this much other than you."

"Me and the devil, we must know each other, then."

I shake my head. "Frankly, I'm surprised anyone who knows the devil is willing to admit it."

"It is worse to know him and give nothing away. No?"

"Are you talking about your friend, that former idol—"

"She is not my friend. I never met her."

"Sorry, Lee, is that her name . . . ?"

"Ai-lee you mean. I-L-E-E. Sounds like 'Eileen' without the *n*."

"I take it you saw her on the news getting carted away in handcuffs?"

"After all this time, she looks the same. I had a postcard of her in my notebook in high school, did I tell you? I feel like I have known her my entire life. Until her face appeared on TV. Funny how wrong we can be about the people we think we know."

"It sounds like your producer didn't see it coming either, and he got a memo about it ahead of time."

"This will be the end of him. End of us too, maybe."

I shake my head. "That sounds like wishful thinking, because the answer is nope."

"Pardon?"

"People love a tragedy almost as much as they like a comedy. Ever notice that the best novels never have happy endings? Shakespeare, Murakami, Tolstoy. Madness or despair, take your pick."

"I do not like to read."

"Then there's a second reason why I didn't try harder to be with you, then, now isn't there?"

Duri squints, trying to register the possibility. "But The Band?"

"Untouchable. Sins past, present, and future, all will be forgotten. Think about it. You guys were the target of a bombing. During an awards show for which you were breaking multiple records, no less. By a disgruntled woman that you might've replaced but never met and did not know, a woman who, if she escapes death or lifelong damnation, will nevertheless be pegged as a misanthrope, a man-hater with a long and sordid history of trying to take down male idols. First Gun, who most certainly deserved it, then you guys, who most certainly did not. Americans who didn't know your names yesterday or couldn't tell the five of you apart will most certainly have heard of you by tomorrow morning, I guarantee you that."

A snort escapes Duri's sinuses. "Is this good news or bad news?"

"Also, no one's dead, last I checked. It doesn't get any better than this!"

"Did they say how she did it?"

I extract my phone, ignoring the half dozen missed calls from Luc, but there are no notifications delineating the mechanisms by which a little girl, an immigrant-fugitive beauty with the mind of a poet working a catering job, managed to blow up the main stage at the Dolby Theatre. "We'll know by the morning," I predict. "If you're still here."

Duri looks at me and blinks. "I am going somewhere?"

I would like to keep him forever, in my pocket or my room or even here, on the inhospitable sand, to feed that hole I see, so familiar I can tell you all the contours and grooves but not where it ends or where it leads. I'd like to mommy him until he comes, receive him in my hand or my belly or wherever the hell he wants, love him long enough to be over him, to falter under the disappointment of who he really is, what he is capable of, and afterward be able to say that I, for once, could see the future and walked into it anyway because I wanted to, and it was worth it. Instead I say, "Yes. Here is the part of the story where you leave me."

The corners of his mouth crawl upward. He thinks this is a game. "What happens if I do not?"

I point behind me. "You take PCH up, you'll hit LAX in twenty. If you turn right when you start seeing planes and then take any of those streets north, you'll find yourself in Hollywood. If you leave now, by the time you get there, the FBI will probably be done with all their questioning. I don't care how much of a national security threat they think this was, they're never going to be able to detain celebrities overnight. By then The Band members will probably also be picking up their phones. Call one of them. Call all of them. Your appearance will be the best news they've seen all night."

Duri glances back at the water as if the sea is another alternative, says nothing.

"You and the devil," I tell him. "The first time you two meet, he gives you this pitch: 'I'll give you the world, but you're going to have to be its slave.' What do you say?"

At this, Duri grins. "Fuck it," he yells.

"Exactly." I get up and walk toward Luc's Volvo waiting where I left it. Before I drive off, I look back at the sand. There's Duri, standing, facing the water, as if still making up his mind. For his sake and mine, I don't linger before going back the way I came.

Epilogue/Aftermath

You know how in the movies, after the final scene fades to black, the ones that are "based on a true story" always have the same white text pop up on the screen, telling you what happened after? Sometimes it'd be good and occasionally it'd be a punch to the gut, but either way, it forced you to stay a little longer and read the damn script and receive the closure we apparently cannot live without.

I am no movie producer, just a therapist moonlighting as a mistress, so I will tell you what I know for sure and leave the rest up to your imagination.

In an impromptu livestream video during the wee hours following the bombing, a disheveled Min with smudged eyeliner and bare lips stares wearily at the camera before opening his mouth, only to close it again. Behind him, a heavily pleated pair of griege hotel curtains stand with the polyester couch cushions to match. Before the dribble of increasingly hysterical viewer comments can start to ask if they are maybe watching a hostage video, Gwangju steps into the frame, hair wet and PJs already on, flannel and a vast baby blue interrupted only by smattering of sheep. For a moment, Min's face looks relaxed, as if it's impossible to stay mad at the world and behold a grown man in its most adorable sleepwear. Yoojin's characteristic tenor calls out from behind the camera, "It's on already?" before Jae's well-inked hands, cradling a flimsy carton of ramen, announce his arrival before the rest of him enters the corner of the screen.

"We are—" Min begins, but then stops. "We're—"

"The Band," offers Gwangju.

"I was going to say alive," the lead says, his smile shrunken and sad. "But I like your answer better."

"It's unclear which one of you is more obvious," Jae snorts between slurps of noodle, just as Gwangju replies, "That's why they call me 'Daddy.'"

"No one calls you that," Yoojin's disembodied voice declares. But then, a reconsider: "Do they?"

Gwangju grins at the camera. "Wouldn't you like to know?" It's unclear whether he is talking to the audience or Yoojin himself—a mystery that will spawn a sizable literature of fan theories followed by an equally sizable body of fan fiction.

"Fans," Min announces, following the Genius's gaze but refusing to imitate his facial expression, "I know it's late and there are a lot of conflicting news reports of what happened, but we wanted to jump online to show you that we're okay."

Maybe all idols instinctively understand that their existence, by definition, hinges ever so precariously on those who idolize them, but you have to give it to these guys: On the worst night of their lives, they're no less dedicated to their followers than on any other. Short of ensuring their own life and limb, each member's next immediate thought appears to always be of their fandom, which now, more than ever, seems more like a phantom limb they're destined to carry around everywhere than a separate entity of people.

"Are we okay, though?" Jae wants to know, his innocence his sword, so cutting that everyone in the room seems to bleed a little.

Min looks at the camera, as if every screen is a mirror on the wall.* Gwangju stares at Jae, who appears to be reading the steam still rising from his bowl for signs and wonders. Only Yoojin's voice, small and distant, emanates from behind: "Who says we have a choice in the matter." A statement dressed up as a question and is anything but.

Before the ensuing silence can break the internet, a phone pings. Four, actually, a veritable quartet of dings reminiscent of C major. Min squints at his device. His eyes, still smudged, start to resemble a raccoon's, enlarged and just a little unhinged. Gwangju, for the second time that night, calls out to Yesu (Jesus), either in gratitude or disbelief. English-speaking commentators think Yoojin and Jae might be calling out to the devil when their "hell" ring out at the same time, but native Korean speakers are quick to point out what they really said was "heol (헐)." Min stands up, as if he can see the future or at least prepare for its landing. On cue, a knock, *tip-tap-TAP*.

"Fans, we have to go," he says. His body blurs across the screen. An outsized hand briefly covers the camera. We hear a door opening before the display shutters to black. What happens next is a future even I don't have access to.**

Instead, here's what I can verify.

Ilee: Because of her international flight risk, our poetess spent five months, three weeks, and one day in jail before her high-profile trial captivated American audiences at a level of obsession we hadn't seen since the O. J. trial. That's when things got tricky. Without a single dead body to atone for, public rancor against her was hard to stoke, although it was not for a lack of trying. The Los Angeles County DA,

---

*If every screen is a mirror on the wall, the real question is whether they're the magic kind that can predict the present and near future or the carnival funhouse types that merely distort.

**Not yet anyway.

a recent transplant from the San Bernardino office named Loyle, spent the first week of the trial parading Cedars-Sinai emergency room doctors through the courtroom to relive, with plenty of photos and obsessive detail, the technique required to remove carpenter nails from a half dozen forearms and feet—a radiologically compelling symposium for the medical community, no doubt, but one that, to the lay audience and jury, felt a bit like an old *ER* episode without George or Juliana or an iota of sexual tension.

Week two: people tuned in for the celeb appearances. Those with no physical injuries to report did the most hand-wringing, listing the insomnia and pill addiction and codependent relationships with their therapists as prime evidence that what they lacked in visible battle wounds, they made up for in despair in the aftermath of the bombing. Things quickly fell apart during the cross-examination, when Ilee's lawyer extracted with a practically surgical precision their preexisting drug usage and comorbid mental health conditions that competed with everything Ilee committed—sorry, *allegedly* committed—for causality.

The moment of bipartisan solemnity came when two amputees took turns taking the stand: a songwriter who had lost his right arm from the elbow down, followed by the wife of a famous rapper who had given up a trifecta of toes. The writer spoke of his phantom limb fondly but with such calm indifference—he was married, with grown children and ambidexterity; his life, as a result, failed to change considerably in the absence of a forearm—that we all walked away wondering if we needed two arms at all (as long as we, too, were hitched, with progeny old enough to play by themselves and a vocation that could be executed single-handedly).

In contrast, the rapper's wife, all fire and brimstone, denounced the Korean government's failure to track its own fugitives, the FBI's general inability to foresee the future, private security firms' useless metal detectors, the Recording Academy's choice of caterer, her own husband for bringing her to the damn show. She did not speak to Ilee directly but rather referred to her repeatedly as "That Woman," taking a cue from a former president's own time on the stand, perhaps. Where she lost public sympathy was when she bemoaned that none of her Stella McCartney shoes fit. No one took her claims of suffering seriously and instead took to the internet to create all sorts of memes for the First World Amputee Problems Club, of which she became its unwitting chair.

Perhaps sensing that the public's identification with these victims was not the reliable calling card he originally assumed it'd be, the DA, mid-trial, switched his approach and instead opted for a different version of great television: the how'd-she-do-it mystery. Consider *American Crime Story* or *Titanic* or *Narcos* or anything about WWII, or WWI for that matter. We all know how these things end. Truly, the ending is the least-interesting part because what we really want to know is how it went down, who else was there, what they were wearing and eating, and who they were fucking. Also, assigning blame is terribly fun if not absolutely necessary. By week three, our man Loyle was done calling witnesses to the stand and ready to move on to a bevy of forensic experts whose side hustles consulting for a certain genre of TV shows (*Law & Order, CSI*, the occasional PBS special) made them uniquely aware of how to talk about science and physics and data without boring the masses in the room.

The rapper's wife was right: the metal detectors and background checks were exercises in futility when it came to preventing this type of lone-wolf attack, which historically tends to be done by those with no priors and a knack for googling things. Ilee, they suspected, like the Tsarnaev brothers before her, looked up the directions on how to make a pressure-cooker bomb on the internet either immediately prior to or shortly after applying to the catering company that had been the de facto provider for all three major awards shows in LA (music, television, movies) for the past two decades (like any other bureaucratic institution, awards shows were rabid followers of the status quo).

Interesting fact #1: Caterers are not in the habit of bringing pressure cookers to events, given that they precook almost all food in stoves or ovens ahead of time.

Interesting fact #2: Despite the previous fact, no one notices when an Instant Pot shows up in a commercial kitchen unasked for and unannounced because it's a kitchen, and there are over a hundred chefs working, plus three times that many servers and five thousand palates with varying degrees of tolerance for gluten, dairy, salt, sugar, and anything with a mom. Remember change blindness and the gorilla in the basketball game? Things that don't belong show up all the time and go unnoticed unless someone's looking for it.

Interesting fact #3: Instant Pot, God bless the Chinese guy who invented it, is not your average pressure cooker. The lower PSI, monitored by a microprocessor that auto-adjusts temperature, heat, and time; the safety latch; the smart lid; the quick-release steam valve— Dr. Robert Wang apparently knew what he was doing when he dumped $300K of his life savings and eighteen months of unemployment during the global 2008 recession into creating a kitchen appliance that allowed domestic goddesses everywhere to stop having to plan ahead for dinner.

When our poetess dumped two pounds of black powder—a homemade recipe of sulfur and carbon oxidized by potassium nitrate, which made it past the metal detectors, no problem—and a handful of nails, screws, and washers that she managed to MacGyver from various kitchen cabinets on the scene into the inner chamber of America's latest cult appliance (which she had left behind inside one of the cabinets a week earlier during a reconnaissance trip), she did not feature these bells and whistles into the physics of her little homemade explosive. She was not a domestic goddess; she had never used an Instant Pot before and thus could not appreciate its many bonus features and what they would do to the pressure-cooker bomb instructions she read online. Cooking, itself a form of chemistry, survives on substituting one ingredient for another, no? Luckily for everyone involved, some forms of combustion demand more precision than others.

To avoid tempting you to try something similar at home in the event you find yourself in a similar spot as Ilee—a woman at the end of herself, interested only in going out with a bang—we will not revisit the precise mechanisms of how she fashioned, reputedly, her DIY explosive. No cameras were allowed in the courtroom anyway, so the only people who got a firsthand lesson on deadly new uses for old things were the judge, jury, witnesses, reporters, and varied friends and family members of those directly involved. Loyle, Mr. DA himself, briefly wondered mid-testimony if perhaps, in prosecuting this woman, he was making it too easy for someone else to follow in her footsteps and correct her mistakes. Still, like other lawyers before him, he was more interested in winning than in saving the world.

Ilee, hours before the ceremony, (supposedly) deposited her hacked Instant Pot below the raised platform on the theater's stage and set her cell phone timer to four minutes after the scheduled start of the show. In other words, immediately prior to the end of The Band's opening song. *Beep, spark, boom.* Somewhere between the smart lid and quick-release valve—add-ons Al-Qaida did not take into consideration when they released their manual on pressure-cooker explosives several months before Robert Wang perfected the art of instant cooking—the combustion crackled where it should have obliterated, leaving those in the audience an excuse to live another day, even if it's without a forearm or a trio of toes.

The evidence against our poet, though, was ultimately circumstantial: There were security cameras everywhere, but not inside the kitchen, where no one famous ever entered and thus no monitoring of shenanigans was ever needed. The stage cameras, of which there were four, did not start recording until immediately prior to the start of the show. No prints emerged on the recovered shredded pieces of Instant Pot because no one in this story is that much of an idiot. Sure, a subpoena of Ilee's credit card transactions did show a purchase of the exact same model of Instant Pot online as the one used for the crime, but market statistics quickly demonstrated that said appliance was the most popular kitchen buy of the last three years; half the courtroom had one.

Here's the clincher: Pinocchio himself, when called by the prosecution, refused to speak ill of his former protégé and instead offered all variety of alternative explanations for the growing number of coincidental events unveiled during discovery. A subpoena of his headquarters' own security footage revealed grainy videos of Ilee— or a woman who resembles Ilee; thanks to outgroup homogeneity effects, this could be any small Asian woman of indeterminate age in a bucket hat—depositing an envelope underneath his door after hours. Flight records confirmed that our defendant made a prolonged trip to the motherland using an alias and fake passport at this same time, and CCTV footage revealed that she visited only two locations during the entirety of her stay: her parents' home in Ilsan and her former music production company. And although the poison-pen letter was itself long gone, Pinocchio repeated its contents for the jury. Whether it was on purpose or not, he feigned only confusion at its words, offering no interpretations for what "coming for your second baby" meant, no matter how many different times Loyle worded the question. When the judge ruled Ilee's previous blackmailing conviction inadmissible by virtue of it having taken place in a South Korean court—for once ethnocentrism did us all a favor—this effectively hobbled Loyle's efforts at drawing a squiggly line at motive, connecting Pinocchio leaving three tumescent girls alone with a powerful man in a foreign nightclub with the cascade of increasingly traumatic aftershocks culminating in a suicide, an escape, and now finally, a payback.

To get around this problem, Loyle tried one final Hail Mary by calling Kimme as his last witness. But she bore so little resemblance to her former idol self that the K-pop devotees in the jury and audience gasped a little when she took the stand. Kimme heard the collective sucking in of stale courtroom air and let out a snort, the universal language of a woman with no more fucks left to give. Loyle, because he was either rather oblivious or quite cruel, projected the last existing tabloid photo of the girl group from outside Le Cinq to remind everyone else who they were looking at: Kimme, in the middle, had her narrow hips unnaturally cocked at an angle to expose both what lies below and sits on top, looking like a sexy flamingo, all leg and suggestibility; Ilee, to the right, was gripping her bandmate by the waist like a sober friend, her pose as unremarkable as a designated driver at a party overrun by drunks. Only S, to their left, was staring off into some distant point beyond the camera, transfixed on whatever it is that's just beyond reach.

Loyle peered into his witness's face, as if trying to search-and-rescue something alive from this detritus of a woman. Unlike the golden calves of yore that people used to worship, modern-day idols tended to be molded from flesh and bone and were thus tragically better at depreciation. Kimme, whose exposed proportions resembled overleavened dough—which, left to rise too long, always deflates on itself and crusts a little—proved this better than anyone. She spoke of her quiet life in a remote town known only for its willow-lined shores and aging population but was otherwise so unremarkable that no one in the room could remember its name long enough to even google its geolocation.

At this point, Ilee looked at Pinocchio, who looked around the courtroom as if searching for someone else to blame for the lengths these girls have gone to escape—by death or derangement or hiding.

Finding no one, he sighed and forced himself to behold the remains of his firstborns before him, barely recognizable because somehow he managed to try both too hard and not hard enough. Although this was not the lesson Loyle wanted to teach his rapt audience, this was the only one he was allowed, as every attempt he made to retrieve a meaningful detail from Kimme about these girls' last days together as a K-pop group, thanks to the woman on trial, was met with one objection or another on the grounds that it was leading or not relevant or prejudicial or speculation or hearsay. So Kimme practiced jaw exercises with her many reps of opening and closing her mouth while our dear DA practiced not losing his goddamn mind.

For reasons even I don't fully know, The Band members themselves were never called to the stand. Maybe Lady Justice's blindfold is less reliable than we thought and even prosecutors are not immune to the consideration fame and fortune afford people. Maybe they were never going to say anything Pinocchio didn't already reveal—or fail to—himself. Likely their presence or absence wouldn't have made a difference: It took the jury two days, but eventually they came back with the anticipated verdict. Not guilty.

Ilee looked a little disappointed. No smile, no tears, not even a goddam cackle. Then again, what's a second chance to a person who thought herself done with everything?

Pinocchio's face, in contrast, conjured up Geppetto on Christmas fucking morning. You would've thought he won the lottery twice. In a weird, twisted sense, he won something better, something that money can't seem to buy, though it's never for lack of trying: exoneration from guilt, of what he could've, would've, should've done if he were to relive his life before The Band and do it differently.

If we could all be so lucky.

The Band, like the Beatles before them, never actually went away, and if anything, became immortal. Thanks to the trial and its round-the-clock coverage, Americans who didn't know them already came to know them by name and discovered, much to their delight, that the teenyboppers were right after all: Their music was infectious in the best way possible, timeless and heartbreaking and very, very catchy. Like, disturbingly so. Really, it wouldn't surprise me if some tightly controlled neuroscientific research on the precise configurations of musical chords that the mesolimbic reward centers of the brain find most addicting went into their latest tunes. To this end, Pinocchio did hold true to his promise to Duri and gave The Band a second life: citing security reasons, the members themselves never performed live again but instead relied on their ever-customizable avatars to do what they did, only better, faster, longer, and more frequently, as robots are in the habit of doing.

The idea, of course, is that all five members are living somewhere, finally free to move on to ordinary lives after having been spared twice—first, from death, thanks to an Instant Pot that proved itself to be no ordinary pressure cooker, and second, from the expectation chained to their talent, thanks to the kind of AI technology that scares the shit out of everyone except those who depend lovingly on it.

There is also the other possibility: that the CGI version of at least one member is all we've got remaining of him because I left him alone near the ocean on a night when his universe almost ended, knowing full well who he was and what he might be capable of, walking away because I needed him, wanted him, to be better and tricked myself into believing that we somehow dwelled in a world where people turned into whatever others demanded they become.

Duri, Duri. You better be out there somewhere.

If only I think, and therefore you are.

Annotated Bibliography

Chapter 1

Chang, Iris. *The Rape of Nanking: The Forgotten Holocaust of World War II*. New York: Basic Books, 2014.
See this book for the full story on the Rape of Nanking and the Nazi in question.

Chapter 3

Roupenian, Kristen. "Cat Person." *The New Yorker* (December 2017): https://www.newyorker.com/magazine/2017/12/11/cat-person.
Le Guin, Ursula K. "The Ones Who Walk Away from Omelas." New York: Harper Perennial, 2017.

Chapter 4

Seghers, M. J., J. J. Longacre, and G. A. DeStefano. "The golden proportion and beauty." *Plastic and Reconstructive Surgery* 34, no. 4 (1964): 382–386.
See this article for more on the golden ratio.
Cialdini, Robert B., Richard J. Borden, Avril Thorne, Marcus Randall

Walker, Stephen Freeman, and Lloyd Reynolds Sloan. "Basking in reflected glory: Three (football) field studies." *Journal of Personality and Social Psychology* 34, no. 3 (1976): 366–375.

See this article for a classic study on BIRGing.

Chapter 5

Tovée, Martin J., Doug S. Maisey, Joanne L. Emery, and Piers L. Cornelissen. "Visual cues to female physical attractiveness." *Proceedings of the Royal Society of London Series B: Biological Sciences* 266, no. 1415 (1999): 211–218.

Lassek, William D., and Steven J. C. Gaulin. "Evidence supporting nubility and reproductive value as the key to human female physical attractiveness." *Evolution and Human Behavior* 40, no. 5 (2019): 408–419.

There are many studies documenting how you can tell a woman's fertility by just looking. These articles are two paradigmatic examples of this.

Chapter 6

Singh, Devendra. "Female mate value at a glance: Relationship of waist-to-hip ratio to health, fecundity and attractiveness." *Neuroendocrinology letters* 23, no. 4 (2002): 81–91.

Psychologists, like the rest of the world, disagree on many things, but one thing they do seem to agree on is a woman's ideal waist-to-hip ratio. This article reviews some of the key literature on WHR.

Chapter 7

Simons, Daniel J., and Christopher F. Chabris. "Gorillas in our midst: Sustained inattentional blindness for dynamic events" *Perception* 28, no. 9 (1999): 1059–1074.

Simons, Daniel. "But Did You See the Gorilla? The Problem With Inattentional Blindness." *Smithsonian* magazine, September 2012, https://www.smithsonianmag.com/science-nature/but-did-you-see-the-gorilla-the-problem-with-inattentional-blindness-17339778/
For the full story on the Invisible Gorilla, see the above.

Improbable Research. "Ig Noble Prize Winners." Accessed April 1, 2020. https://improbable.com/ig/winners/.

Thébaud, Sarah, Sabino Kornrich, and Leah Ruppanner. "Good housekeeping, great expectations: Gender and housework norms." *Sociological Methods & Research* 50, no. 3 (2021): 1186–1214.

Hughes, Brent L., Nicholas P. Camp, Jesse Gomez, Vaidehi S. Natu, Kalanit Grill-Spector, and Jennifer L. Eberhardt. "Neural adaptation to faces reveals racial outgroup homogeneity effects in early perception." *Proceedings of the National Academy of Sciences* 116, no. 29 (2019): 14532–14537.
See this paper for evidence on outgroup homogeneity effects.

Chapter 9

Diener, Edward, and Shigehiro Oishi. "Money and happiness: Income and subjective well-being across nations." In *Culture and Subjective Well-being*, edited by Ed Diener and Eunkook M. Suh, 185–218. Cambridge: MIT Press, 2000.
As this paper suggests, money does make you happy, after all.

Aronson, Elliot, Ben Willerman, and Joanne Floyd. "The effect of a pratfall on increasing interpersonal attractiveness." *Psychonomic Science* 4, no. 6 (1966): 227–228.

Helmreich, Robert, Elliot Aronson, and James LeFan. "To err is humanizing sometimes: Effects of self-esteem, competence, and a pratfall on interpersonal attraction." *Journal of Personality and Social Psychology* 16, no. 2 (1970): 259.
These unpack the Pratfall effect.

Chentsova-Dutton, Yulia E., Jeanne L. Tsai, and Ian H. Gotlib. "Further evidence for the cultural norm hypothesis: Positive emotion in depressed and control European American and Asian American women." *Cultural Diversity and Ethnic Minority Psychology* 16, no. 2 (2010): 284.

This paper discusses depression, Asians, and who laughs at what.

Gross, James J., and Robert W. Levenson. "Emotion elicitation using films." *Cognition & Emotion* 9, no. 1 (1995): 87–108.

Chapter 12

Slovic, Paul. "The more who die, the less we care." In *The Feeling of Risk*, edited by Terre Satterfield, C. K. Mertz, and Paul Slovic, 97–106. New York: Routledge, 2013.

This paper covers the Collapse of Compassion studies.

Chapter 14

Dutton, Donald G., and Arthur P. Aron. "Some evidence for heightened sexual attraction under conditions of high anxiety." *Journal of Personality and Social Psychology* 30, no. 4 (1974): 510.

For a full explanation of the original rickety bridge study, see the paper above.

Chapter 15

Gray, Kurt, and Daniel M. Wegner. "Blaming God for our pain: Human suffering and the divine mind." *Personality and Social Psychology Review* 14, no. 1 (2010): 7–16.

If you ever wondered about the link between God and suffering, read Kurt Gray and Daniel Wegner's work on the divine mind.

Chapter 17

Wallace, David Foster. *Infinite Jest*. London: Hachette UK, 2011.
David Foster Wallace, the OG of writing about depression and its metaphors, famously compared suicide with jumping from a burning building.

Acknowledgments

Thank you to:

Emmy Higdon Nordstrom, whose editorial eye, sensitivity, and insight I will forever be thankful for; and Loan Le, the kind of brilliantly talented editor my best dreams are made of. You two made this book a better read and made me a better writer.

BTS and ARMY, who, on top of changing the course of music (and human) history, showed me—along with the rest of the universe—that there is nothing quite as powerful as a group of people brought together by the singularity of their passion and the dedication of their pursuit.

My parents, who never tired of telling me stories long before I ever figured out how to write one myself. My sister, Eleanor, who put up with my antics long before I learned how to sublimate them into something more productive, like this book, and continues to support me in things big and small.

Eugene Hwang, who helped me with the original Hangul and proved to be better than both Google Translate and Papago combined.

Luke, Everest, and Josiah. I started and finished the original draft of this novel in 2020, when the world fell apart and everyone found themselves stuck inside, so the fact that this book exists is a testament to their greatness as housemates (also: husband and sons).

And to everyone else I forgot but will invariably recall later: you know who you are. Hopefully. (If not, I promise I'll remember by my next book.)

About the Author

Christine Ma-Kellams is a Harvard-trained cultural psychologist, Pushcart-nominated fiction writer, and first-generation American. As an associate professor of psychology at San Jose State University, her empirical work on the emotional lives and biases of Asians and white people have not only been published in premier academic journals but also widely covered in *GQ, Esquire*, the *Boston Globe, New York* magazine, *Huffington Post*, and *Psychology Today*. Rowman & Littlefield published her textbook, *Cultural Psychology*. Her short stories, essays, and interviews have been featured in over three dozen literary magazines and news outlets, including *Prairie Schooner*, the *Rumpus, Catapult, ZYZZYVA*, the *Kenyon Review, Monkeybicycle*, the *Rupture, Electric Literature, Southern Humanities Review*, the *Saturday Evening Post*, the *Wall Street Journal, Salon, HuffPost*, the *Chicago Tribune*, and elsewhere. You can find her in person in one of California's coastal cities or online at christinema-kellams.com.